LAVENDER AND LIES

PORT DANBY COZY MYSTERY #11

LONDON LOVETT

CHAPTER 1

$\mathcal{M}$y feet practically pranced along the sidewalk, an unusually enthusiastic stride for a Monday morning, but the beautiful day required it. For me there was nothing more invigorating and uplifting than a crisp fall day with an azure blue sky. The air was filled with a brisk salty scent and the comforting aroma of Les's pumpkin spice coffee. Monday or not, there was just no way to be gloomy when we were surrounded by swirls of autumn. It was late enough in the season that most of the brilliant yellows and oranges had darkened to reds and browns. Soon, most of the color would be gone, leaving behind only the hearty verdant green of the tall pines on the outskirts of town. Then, winter would rear its frosty head and trigger our instinctual quest for coziness. Briggs always found it humorous that I looked forward to the inconvenient ice and wind of winter, but as I'd explained to him many times, bitter cold always brought with it the promise of hot cocoa, roaring fires and cuddles under thick, flannel blankets. And that was never a bad thing. Even he had to admit the cuddling under thick blankets was a definite check on the positive side when it came to winter.

My tall, perpetually handsome neighbor, Dash, came around the corner from the Coffee Hutch just as I reached the door to my flower shop. Kingston recognized him instantly and hopped along the sidewalk toward him in hopes of garnering a treat.

Dash stopped and stared down at my pushy crow. "Sorry, buddy, this extra coffee is for your mom."

I squeaked a little in excitement. "I hoped that was the case, only I didn't want to assume and make an—well, you know." I reached for the hot cup of coffee. Fragrant molecules of clove, cinnamon and nutmeg clung to the curl of steam hovering over the cup. I took a sip and made the obligatory sigh. "So yummy." I peered up at Dash. He was wearing a blue and green flannel shirt, a good look for him. Although, everything looked nice on him. Now that Briggs had finally accepted that Dash and I were friends, Dash and I had grown closer again. He was, after all, my neighbor, and frankly, there was nothing more disagreeable and awkward than disliking your neighbor. Dash had brutally betrayed Briggs some years earlier and I would never feel quite the same about him, but it was much more pleasant being on friendly terms. Life was just too short for anxiety and dismay.

I took one more sip. "Les is the king of coffee roasters."

I turned back to unlock the door. Kingston elbowed, or winged, past us and headed for his perch in the shop window. The entire store was bathed with the perfumed scent of gardenias. Ryder and I had spent the last week making arrangements for a wedding, and the gardenias were what I liked to call the main event in the bridal bouquets.

It wasn't an easy week, considering just how fragrant gardenias are, especially if you're cutting, pruning and manipulating them to fit in a bouquet. My hypersensitive nose prompted me to leave the shop to clear my head at least five times. Fortunately, my perfectly wonderful floral assistant, Ryder, stepped in whenever the perfume overwhelmed me.

Dash had put down his coffee to search for the treat can on the work island. "I think if I walk out of here without giving that bird a snack, he'll shun me forever."

I smiled. "You're probably right. King is very good at the whole cold shoulder routine. The can is on the second shelf, below the ribbon spools." I pulled off my coat and carried my things back to the office. I turned on my computer and headed back out.

Dash was talking to Kingston, letting him know that he would always carry a treat in his pocket from now on, for emergencies. The crow was already far too absorbed in breaking open the peanut shell to hear the promise.

"So it's official," Dash said, sounding slightly sad.

"What? That my bird really only cares about treats?"

He laughed quietly. "No, I was talking about Britney. She's going back to Paris. She got the internship with the big pastry chef." Dash wasn't the type of person to frown, but he was definitely close to it. Dash and Elsie's niece, Britney, a beautiful, young woman and extremely talented baker, had been dating for months. The best word to describe the relationship was tumultuous. Britney had come on far too strong in the beginning, and it had scared Dash off a bit. He was convinced he didn't have deep feelings for her, and his occasional indifference to her had riled Elsie up good. I'd found myself, far too often, in the center of the entire mess. But now, it seemed Dash was genuinely sad to see Britney go.

I walked over to him and patted his arm. "Guess it's that old saying —you don't know what you have until it's gone."

He nodded. "That pretty much sums it up. Still, this is a great opportunity for her, and we're going to keep in touch. Who knows, it might not be the end for us. Might just be a new beginning for her."

"Well put."

The bell on the door clanged. Normally, I would have been surprised to see Kate Yardley, owner of the vintage clothing boutique, walking into the flower shop on a Monday morning, but it was easy to surmise that she had spotted Dash walking in behind me. Kate was beautiful, fashionable, successful and slightly standoffish. We had never become good friends, but we occasionally spoke like familiar acquaintances. She was also interminably in love with Dash. They had dated briefly and had seen each other off and on, but he was not inter-ested in anything serious or permanent. Kate, on the other hand, was in constant pursuit of something very permanent, namely a husband.

In the past year, she had been in and out of engagements with four different men. I wasn't sure whether to consider it absurd or sad. I couldn't understand why she had such a difficult time with it all, but her ongoing obsession with Dash probably wasn't helping matters.

This morning, Kate's attire was unusually subdued. She'd forgone the usual mod, flashy clothing for a simple pair of jeans and a pale blue sweater. Her only nod to the vintage style she always wore so well was a giant pair of silver hoops in her ears.

She shuffled in on short black boots, brushed back the hair from her shoulder and glanced instantly at my other visitor. "Oh, Dash, hello, I didn't see you there," she said lightly, along with a not so subtle flutter of her lashes.

"Morning, Kate, good to see you," Dash said politely back.

"Hello, Pink, beautiful morning isn't it?" Now I was sure her visit was a scheme to see Dash. She never called me Pink, and she certainly never brought up the topic of weather. She was not big on frill or friendly conversation, but it seemed today I was in for a treat. She hopped up on a stool in front of the work island.

"What can I get for you, Kate?" I asked. "Ryder planted some fresh herbs in decorative pots—" I was just about to point them out on the shelf across the way when she jumped right into her main purpose for the visit.

"Actually, I just wanted to let you know that you might have a new customer this afternoon." She spoke loudly enough to make sure Dash, who was giving Kingston another peanut, could hear. Her eyes flicked his direction as she spoke to make sure he hadn't left.

"That's nice to know," I said. "A friend of yours? I'll be sure to give her a special deal."

"It's a man," she corrected briskly, with another glance Dash's direction. "My new boyfriend, Lionel." Her voice carried across the room. She leaned in as if she was going to lower her voice and tell me something in confidence (which would have been even weirder than her calling me Pink). Only she never lowered her voice. In fact, she spoke clearly and loudly to make sure every syllable reached Dash's ears. "He's just moved into a massive colonial mansion in Chesterton.

You know, the expensive area, with all the big houses and million dollar estates?" she asked. "It overlooks Chesterton Bay."

"Yes, I know the neighborhood. Very nice. He must do well." I decided to play along with the new best friend status she'd invented between us.

"He's very wealthy." She smoothed her hair down on one side and turned just enough in the process to get another quick look at Dash. For someone who had a new, rich boyfriend, she certainly was spending a good deal of time gawking at Dash.

"That's nice. What does he do?" I asked. It was a perfectly logical follow up question, but it seemed to have her flummoxed. But I wasn't terribly surprised, considering Kate went through men like most people went through socks. It was entirely possible she hadn't known this man Lionel long enough to even find out his last name, let alone his profession.

"He's in trade or exports or something like that." She waved off any specifics with a flutter of her long, pink nails. I'd found, in my first decade in the adult world, that when someone said they were involved in trade or exports, it usually meant they were either just trying to sound important or they were up to something shady. I was hoping, for Kate's sake, it was the former.

Kate reached into her shiny leather clutch and pulled out her phone. It was tucked inside a rhinestone protective case. Her long nails slid over the screen. "Lionel is camera shy, but I managed to sneak one picture of him. This was inside his dining room. It's still empty. He ordered a French antique dining table, but it's coming all the way from Europe." She shoved the phone out for me to see.

There was no denying that Lionel was handsome, with a strong chin and straight nose. There was also no denying that he was probably in his mid to late forties, with graying around the temples and strands of white in his thick, wavy hair. I'd never asked but I always assumed Kate was around my age. I supposed the age difference was easy to overlook when it came with a mansion. Although, from the bits I could see, this particular mansion needed some heavy duty rehab.

"I'll see you both later," Dash said as he headed toward the exit.

"Goodbye, Dash," Kate said with a wave. "By the way, if you see a new silver Porsche zipping through town it belongs to my new friend, Lionel."

Dash nodded. "Good to know." He was trying hard to hide a grin. Kate was making it so comically obvious, it almost didn't seem like her. Not that she was ever subtle when it came to Dash but this partic-ular performance was Oscar worthy.

"Thanks for the coffee," I called to Dash as he slipped out the door to freedom. Something told me my own freedom was just around the corner now that her main reason for the visit had disappeared.

"He's very handsome," I said to her as she put the phone back in her purse. "Like a movie star."

"Isn't he? I've told him that too, that he should be in the movies." My earlier prediction had been correct.

Kate hopped off the stool to leave.

"What makes you think Lionel would be visiting the flower shop?" I asked, realizing she'd never finished her purported reason for the visit.

She stopped her brisk exit long enough to answer. Her earlier chummy smile had faded. She was Kate Yardley again, the woman who barely tolerated me only because I was a shop owner on the same street.

"Oh, that's right. Last night, during our dinner at Marcel's Italian Bistro in Mayfield, he asked me what my favorite flower was. I answered red roses, of course. Just wanted to give you the heads up and please make sure they're fresh. There's nothing more disap-pointing than having red roses wilt and lose petals just days after receiving them." With that, she turned on her short boot heels and left the shop.

CHAPTER 2

*R*yder came out from the office with his lunch bag. "I'm going across the street to have lunch with Lola. I can finish potting that basil when I get back."

I didn't look up from my order pad. "Have a nice lunch."

The romantic relationship between my marvelous assistant, Ryder, and my best friend, Lola, had not hit any of the usual bumps lately and as standby couple's therapist I was relieved. It seemed they had finally found their rhythm, and Ryder had come to love some of Lola's quirks, all traits that made her that much more lovable . . . most of the time, anyhow.

The bell tinkled lightly, slowly, as two elderly women, with heavy purses on their arms and glasses on the tips of their noses, pushed the front door. It was not a terribly heavy door but they struggled none-theless.

I raced around the work island to give them a hand, which was when I noticed one was shuffling along behind a walker. The woman who shuffled in next to her, a hand at her elbow to help move her along, was slightly hunched and had pearl white hair. If I'd had to guess her age, I could confidently state that she had already celebrated her eightieth birthday. The woman with the walker was much tinier, shriveled, for lack of a better word. Her dark eyes had a filmy gray cast to them, but her skin was remarkably fresh and smooth.

"Welcome to Pink's Flowers. How can I help you?" I walked on the woman's other side, worried that my tile floor might prove too slick for her walker, but she managed to inch along without incident.

The woman with the pearl white hair spoke first. She stopped and adjusted her glasses as she looked me over with blue eyes. "You must be Lacey. My friend, Frida, told me I should go to Pink's Flowers and talk to Lacey, the owner. She said you'd be able to help us select flowers for Mary's birthday." She inclined her head toward the woman with the walker. "This is Mary and I'm Katherine, her daughter."

Mary's attention had been grabbed away by the large, black bird in the shop window. She didn't pay any attention to the conversation at hand.

"I can definitely help you with that." I glanced back at the stools in front of the work island and realized I was woefully unprepared for my two customers. I couldn't possibly expect either of them to hop up on a stool.

"I could bring some chairs out from my office so the two of you could sit down and look at catalogs."

Katherine looked at her mother. "Mom, would you like a chair?" she said loudly.

Mary ignored the question and turned back to me. "Why do you still have up your Halloween display?" Her voice was craggy and weak. She looked at her daughter. "Is it still October? I thought it was November. Why are we here? My birthday isn't until November."

"It is November, Mom, and your birthday is in ten days." Both women were talking loudly enough that it unsettled Kingston. He flew down from his perch and trotted across the floor to hide behind the work island.

Mary stared at him as he skittered across the floor, then she turned to her daughter. "I need my nap, Kat. I'm seeing things."

"No, Mom, you're' not. Unless I'm seeing things too." Katherine turned to me. "Frida told me you had a crow, but I must admit, I thought she was kidding with me."

"No, I'm afraid she wasn't. That was Kingston. He gets shy some-times so he's hiding. He won't bother us. Now, how about the chairs?"

"Mom, did you want a chair?" Katherine asked loudly.

Mary shook her head. "No, I'll stand. Want to be ready in case that bird comes flying out of nowhere."

"Lacey says the bird won't bother us," Katherine said clearly and loudly like a teacher giving instructions.

"I don't need a chair. I want lilacs, lavender lilacs," Mary stated emphatically enough to slightly dislodge her top row of teeth. She pushed them back in." She looked at me for the first time since they'd walked inside. "Is this pretty girl the florist? I want lilacs. You should do something about that bird, chase him out with a broom or rake."

I decided to just stick with the flower topic. "I can order lilacs. Are these for table settings?" I turned to Katherine.

Katherine nodded. "Yes. We'll need ten centerpieces."

"I'm going to be ninety-five," Mary stated proudly.

"No, Mom, you're going to be a hundred and five."

I was sure I gasped a little but couldn't stop myself.

"That's impossible." Mary smacked the top of her walker. "No one lives past a hundred."

"Well, you managed it just fine, Mom." Katherine turned back to me with an apologetic smile. "She can be a little stubborn sometimes."

"I can hear, ya know?" Mary barked. "And you're the stubborn one. I want lilacs."

"Yes, Mom, we're getting lilacs." Katherine grinned again. "My father used to bring her lilacs every birthday."

"How wonderful," I said. "They are a lovely flower, and they make great centerpieces. I can spruce them up with some nice greenery. Should I order some white ones too or just the lavender?"

"Just the lavender," Mary blurted before Katherine could comment.

"Let me just get an order pad and we can write this up." I circled around to the back side of the island. Kingston had squeezed himself onto the second shelf, conveniently next to his treat can. It seemed he had decided that the two loud talking customers might just steal off with his goodies.

As I rummaged around for a working pen, Katherine continued talking.

"My mother has lived here, in Port Danby, her entire life. She used to help run the post office."

I finally found a pen that actually had ink, and I carried it along with my order pad to the side they were standing on. As I settled my paper down on the island a thought occurred to me. Mary must have known everyone in town if she worked for the post office. "Mary, did you know Harvard Price, the mayor?"

Mary squinted her cloudy eyes as if that might help her hear better. "Who?"

"Mayor Price, Mom. Harvard Price."

Mary released her white knuckled grip for one second to wave her hand. It was bone white with the exception of numerous brown age spots. "He was always angry. Always grumpy." She scrunched up her face to mimic his grumpiness. It was adorable. "Never liked the man. His son, Fielding, took over the mayor's office in 1935. I voted for Harris Bookman. Never liked the Prices."

My astonishment at her memory must have shown.

"My mom still has an incredible memory for details, especially things that happened long ago. Not so much for everyday things. This morning she came out of her room and forgot to put on her skirt."

"No I didn't," Mary snapped. "And stop talking about me as if I'm not standing right here. Like I'm dead or something."

Katherine rolled her eyes. "Fine, Mom. I won't talk about you until you are actually dead."

Mary curled her fingers around the handles on the walker. "You might go before me." There was a glint of humor in her overcast eyes.

I pressed my fingers against my lips to stifle a smile.

Katherine sighed. "She has not lost her sense of humor either. Now, about the lilacs. We need ten good sized arrangements. We've rented round tables with a six foot diameter, if that helps you."

"Yes it does." I wrote everything down. My mind was still not on work. I had someone standing in my shop, who had actually known

Harvard Price. There were too many questions to ask but one stood out the most.

"Mary, I wonder, you mentioned Fielding Price, Harvard's son. Do you happen to know anything about Jane Price, Harvard's daughter?"

Mary pursed her mouth in thought. "Jane Price?"

"Yes, I believe she was his daughter from a previous marriage." I was giddy with anticipation.

Right then, Kingston trotted back out from behind the counter, stealing Mary's attention away from the Jane Price question. Darn bird. He marched with crow-like purpose to the door, signaling he needed to take a trip around the neighborhood.

"Excuse me," I said to the two women who were completely mesmerized by the crow at the door.

I hurried across to the door and pushed it open. Kingston stepped out into the bright sunlight and turned toward Elsie's bakery. It was his morning routine, clean up crumbs in Elsie's outdoor seating area, fly across to sit on Lola's roof, hoping to get a glimpse of his sweetheart, then it was off to the town square to see what the other birds were up to. He never got close to any of them and preferred to stay at a distance, observing and, most likely, judging. He was like the snooty odd ball in high school who'd decided he was too good to hang with the regular kids. Although, occasionally I'd catch him staring dreamily at a group of crows hanging out on the lawn, and it always made me worry that he might someday decide to take off with his kin. But he always returned and he always seemed to be relieved to be back on his perch nibbling on hard boiled eggs. (Something told me the lack of hard boiled eggs in nature was the deal breaker.)

Katherine laughed briefly as I headed back to the order pad.

"My goodness, he is just like a dog."

I smiled. "Yes, he is," I agreed, then smirked to myself thinking how much Kingston would hate to be compared to a dog. He really considered himself to be a much higher species than the rest of us inhabiting his space.

I finished writing up the order and had nearly forgotten about my earlier enthusiasm to find out more about Jane Price. But Mary hadn't forgotten.

"You should talk to Marty Tate, the lighthouse keeper," Mary spoke up in a creaky, soft tone.

Katherine looked at her with confusion. "Why on earth would Lacey need to talk to Marty?"

"Jane Price." Mary tapped her walker with frustration. "She was asking about Jane Price. You sure are forgetful." Mary turned to me. "Used to be such a scatterbrain when she was a little girl. She'd walk out of the house with two different shoes or sometimes forget them altogether."

Katherine tilted her head at her mother. "Well then, isn't it funny how history repeats itself? Only I wasn't the one who walked out without my skirt this morning, was I?"

"Told you, I didn't forget it. I just didn't want to wear it." It was entertaining to watch them spar. I momentarily wondered if I was looking fifty years into the future at my mom and me but then I worked to steer the conversation back to Jane Price.

"Do you think Marty would know about Jane Price?" I asked Mary.

"No, he's too young," Mary said confidently, and that seemed to be the disappointing end to my quest.

Katherine sighed loudly. "Sorry about that. We won't take up any more of your time."

"I'll get right on the computer to order the lilacs." I pulled the order form off the tablet.

"Marty's mother, Elizabeth, she knew everyone," Mary spoke up sharply. "She was the town busy body but always friendly. She used to give me butter shortbread whenever I stopped by to play with Marty. Like I said, she knew everyone. Maybe Marty will know if she was friends with Jane Price."

I couldn't contain my excitement. For well over two years, I'd been plodding along, looking for tidbits that might help me unfold the mystery around the turn of the century murder of the entire Hawksworth family. It seemed I had my first arrow pointing me in the right direction. Port Danby was a small town, and if what Mary said was true, that Marty's mother Elizabeth knew everybody, then it was entirely possible she knew Jane Price. And with any luck, Marty would know something too. No one was quite sure of Marty's age, but it seemed Mary had played with him as a child. I could only assume he was just over a hundred like Mary. He wouldn't have been alive when Jane Price left town, but maybe he knew something. My trails had all run dry lately, so any tiny sliver of knowledge would be thrilling. My intuition coupled with the evidence I'd uncovered thus far had me theorizing that Jane Price was somehow mixed up with the murder. I just wasn't sure how.

I held the door as my two customers shuffled out complaining to each other about whether or not it was cold enough for a sweater or a coat. It was a good start to the week, a pumpkin spice coffee, a nice birthday order and a helpful suggestion in the Hawksworth murder case. The only thing that might make this week better was an actual murder case. Of course, I wasn't hoping someone would get killed, but I had to admit things had been a bit boring around town lately. A good investigation could spark things up.

CHAPTER 3

After the brisk walk to Franki's Diner, I pinched my cheeks for color before entering. The aroma of chili and onions mingled with the sweet tart fragrance of Franki's freshly baked handheld cinnamon apple pies. They were a delight, and the townsfolk went crazy for them when she trotted them out, fresh and bubbly from the oven, for exactly one month a year. I would venture to say, although never out loud since Elsie might hear, that Franki's handheld cinnamon apple treasures could easily compete with Elsie's baked goods. (And that was saying a lot. Only again, just not aloud.)

Briggs was sitting at our favorite table, a quiet booth with a nice view of the marina. He had removed his coat and loosened his tie. His longish hair was slightly wind rumpled. I paused for just a second to catch my breath. The sight of him usually caused a slight dip in oxygen to my brain. It wasn't a swoon but it was pretty darn close. His bright smile, upon seeing me, nearly made it a full blown swoon. I took another steadying breath and walked toward him.

"I've already ordered. Tomato and grilled cheese, as requested." Briggs leaned back and rested his arm along the top of the vinyl seat. He was smiling at something on my face.

I immediately reached up and rubbed my chin. "Do I have soil on my face? I was potting herbs." I picked up the napkin and started wiping my skin. "Is it on my forehead?"

He shook his head and using the crook of his finger, motioned me to lean toward him over the table. I lowered the napkin and closed my eyes so he could wipe away the dirt. His warm mouth pressed against mine, then he sat back with a chuckle.

"Well, sir, you are a scoundrel. You could have just asked for a kiss. I probably would have obliged."

He laughed again. "Probably?"

"I wouldn't want to seem too eager," I said plainly as I dropped the napkin, crumpled as it was, on my lap.

"No?" he said with a low, teasing voice. His feet slid across and he sandwiched my shoe between his. "That's too bad because eager is my middle name when I see my beautiful assistant and her stunning nose sitting across from me."

I tossed a sugar packet at him. "I stand firmly behind my scoundrel comment. What has you so frolicsome today?"

He laughed again. "Frolicsome? Miss Pinkerton, I think I love you just because you use words like frolicsome. And, I'm sorry if I'm being a scoundrel." He sat back and picked up his glass of water. "It's been slow at work, so I guess I've had more time than usual to daydream about my favorite florist."

I could feel my cheeks darken with a blush, but there was no way to stop it. I sat forward with a teasing smile to match his. "First of all, no need to apologize for being a scoundrel. After all, I never said that was a *bad* thing, did I? And secondly, as long as I'm the aforementioned favorite florist, then daydream away. Just make sure to daydream about me with my curls somewhat tamed and a touch of mascara. I'd hate to look bad in your musings."

He reached across for my hand, which I gladly offered. His grip was always warm and strong and comforting. "You are always beautiful, whether it's in my imagination or sitting right across from me at Franki's Diner or sick on the couch with a bad cold. All right, that last flu you had did make you kind of look like Rudolph the Red Nose Reindeer but in an adorable, vulnerable Bambi kind of way," he added quickly before I could protest.

"Tomato soup with grilled cheese," Franki said as she set a plate and bowl in front of me. "Your burger will be right up, James."

"Franki," I said, before she could turn away. She was wearing her signature beehive, and today she had taken the time to stick in a few resin fall leaf clips to spruce it up. "Could you pull aside one of your marvelous hand pies? I've been craving one all day."

"Sure thing, Lacey." She stepped forward and leaned closer to the table for a chat. "By the way, have you seen Kate's new guy?"

"I have but only in a phone picture. Much to my surprise, she stopped in the shop this morning. Although, I guess it wasn't too big of a surprise because Dash just happened to be there." I knew that statement would catch the ears of the man across from me, but that wasn't the purpose for me stating it. "Kate wanted to let me know he might be stopping in to buy her some roses. I've yet to see him in the flesh. Have you seen him? She mentioned he was wealthy, but she didn't have many specifics on what he did for a living."

A customer at the counter was waving at Franki. She gave the man a nod. "I'll be right with you." She turned back to our table. "They came in for lunch today. He might be rich but he's not a great tipper. But then that isn't unusual. It's always the people who drive up in the luxury SUV with a car filled with kids who leave the table looking as if it's been through a hurricane who you can count on to leave two dollars on a sixty dollar bill." She paused and straightened. "Woo, guess I needed to get that one off my chest. Anyhow, he seems nice. Very distinguished looking. A bit old for Kate but you know our Kate. She seems completely smitten. I just hope it doesn't end up in another heartbreak. She does seem to get attached quickly."

"Wasn't she engaged to the pharmacist?" Briggs asked.

Franki and I both snuffled off his question. "Please, the pharmacist was two engagements ago, James," I said.

"Guess I've been out of the loop." He reached across and took one of my fries.

"Well, let's hope she can keep this one," Franki said. "Seems like he's a nice catch. Apparently, he just purchased the big Colonial mansion overlooking the bay in Chesterton."

"The Palmer house?" Briggs sat up, slightly more interested now. "That place has been in probate for years. The family lives out of state. I'm surprised to hear they finally sold it."

Franki shrugged. "I'm pretty sure that was the place he mentioned. I'll get your burger and snag one of the apple pies for you." She winked at me before leaving.

"So Kate dropped by this morning?" Briggs asked, but I knew he wasn't interested in Kate's visit.

"Yes, she did." I blinked at him over my spoonful of hot tomato soup. "Dash brought me a pumpkin coffee. Kate must have seen him, so naturally, she sashayed into the shop." I blinked at him again to let him know the conversation around this particular topic had ended.

He got the message. "Right. Well, I'm still kind of surprised to hear that this new guy of Kate's was able to buy the Palmer house. So many people have been waiting for that place to go on the market."

"Maybe Lionel has connections," I suggested after swallowing a bite of sandwich.

"Lionel?" he asked.

"That's his name."

Franki returned with the burger. "Looks good, Franki. I'm starved."

Franki slipped me a brown paper bag with a light grease stain and the undeniable aroma of apples and cinnamon. "Here you go. Enjoy."

I grinned up at her. "Thanks, Franki, I plan to."

CHAPTER 4

$\mathcal{I}$t was far too beautiful of a day to head straight back to work, so I walked Briggs to the door of the police station, kissed him goodbye, then turned back to take a brisk stroll along the wharf and marina. My original goal, as stated to my boyfriend in parting, was to walk off the large lunch. The sandwich soup combo was always one of my favorites, but a creamy soup and a buttery sandwich were heavy comfort food. However, my plans to walk off a few calories were quickly doused when I could no longer wait to nibble on the hand pie. The warm, spicy scent of cinnamon coupled with the tangy bite of apple kept calling to me from the inside of the greasy brown bag.

I pulled it out just as I took my first step on the wharf. It seemed seagulls also had a keen sense of smell. I instantly became quite the adored rock star as I sauntered along with my flaky confection. There was no way not to shed a few crumbs of Franki's light, crispy pastry, so my feathered groupies slapped along behind me on rubbery orange feet, cleaning up every morsel.

The brisk breeze flowing in from the navy blue tide had the scent of romance and faraway places. The ocean was always such an extraordinary sight, endless blue glass trimmed with the occasional white frost and the poetic glide of a meandering sailboat. I closed my eyes and listened for the sound of the ocean but realized there was far too much people noise to find the rhythm. The gorgeous blue day, chilly as it was, had brought people out from houses and businesses to partake in some of the beach-y treats being offered along the wharf. A man carrying what appeared to be a sandwich consisting of two waffles and a piece of fried chicken stole my fickle crowd of long beaked fans away. Off they waddled, although something told me the waffles wouldn't be nearly as generous as the flaky crust on my pie.

I decided to head to the marina to take one quick tour of the lovely boats before heading back to work. Some of the boat owners were busy getting their vessels ready for the onslaught of winter, packing deck chairs into storage areas and covering permanent fixtures with canvas tarps. An unfamiliar good-sized luxury cruiser, big and elegant enough that it might even be classified as a yacht (I wasn't well versed in boat categories) bobbed quietly in the second to last slip. It was cleverly named *Funtasy*. The owner seemed to be ignoring the chill hovering over the marina. She was stretched out on a lounge in skin tight, white jeans (even though Labor Day had long since passed). Her auburn hair was streaked with honey highlights, and her lips were slightly swollen, as if she had just had them plumped and filled. The snug zebra print sweater that hugged her curves, along with the oversized round turquoise blue sunglasses and the bright pink drink she sipped from a martini glass all reminded me of an old time movie star, as if Greta Garbo or Joan Crawford had just sailed into Port Danby for a day trip.

I hadn't meant to stare but apparently I'd been obvious. She waved hello before picking up her bright pink drink. I waved shyly back and hurried along. I left the marina and headed along the wharf and suddenly got the distinct feeling I was being watched. I spun around and found that I was indeed being watched, by my bird.

Kingston was perched on the back of one of the many benches on the wharf. He glanced nonchalantly off to the side as if he hadn't even noticed me pass by. He was an expert at playing aloof.

I walked back to him. "I guess there wasn't enough entertainment

19

at the town square," I said to him, loudly enough that several people passing by glanced around to see who I might have been talking to. It was just me, a crazy lady talking to a crow. A few gasps followed as Kingston hopped onto my shoulder and settled in for an easy journey back to the shop.

"Oh my gosh, do you see that, Gary? That crow is sitting on the lady's shoulder," a woman said as we strolled past.

Kingston shifted sideways, using his talons to keep steady and making me thankful for the thickness of my coat. He wanted to catch his last glimpse of the beach before we left the wharf. For a brief period of time, Kingston had spent a lot of time sitting on the pylons of the pier and the rooftops of the wharf shops gazing longingly at the gulls on the beach. I was convinced he'd decided that the life of a seagull was far more grand than the life of a crow (with the exception of Kingston himself. He had it pretty sweet.) I thought he was trying to learn their ways so he could hang with them. After all, they spent a great deal of time scouring goodies from the pier and beach in between naps on the warm sand. It didn't take me too long to figure out that his obsession with the seagulls was not out of envy. It was not because the gulls led a more glamorous life. It was more due to the fact that they were sloppy eaters. All that time, I'd thought he was observing the gulls, trying to learn their habits, when it turned out he was just waiting to swoop in and pick up all the left behind crumbs. Occasionally, I gave my bird more credit than he deserved.

I was just about to leave the beach area altogether when I remembered that Mary had told me to talk to Marty Tate about his mother and her possible friendship with Jane Price. I pulled out my phone and texted Ryder.

"Is the shop busy or can I extend my lunch break another fifteen?"

Ryder wrote right back. "Just helped a customer with some of the potted herbs, and now I've got the place to myself. I haven't seen Kingston. Should we be worried?"

I lifted the phone for a selfie. "Smile, Kingston." I took the picture and sent it.

"Ah ha, I see the two of you are doing your pirate and parrot impression. See you soon."

"I'm going to send this bird to the shop before he destroys my coat. Keep an eye out for him." I texted back.

"Will do."

I swung my arm toward Harbor Lane. "Off you go. Ryder will have a treat for you when you get back." The word treat was all the encouragement he needed. His talons poked my shoulder as he pushed off and headed toward the shop. I, on the other hand, spun around on my heels and headed toward Pickford Lighthouse.

CHAPTER 5

A sporadic breeze that could almost be classified as wind had kicked up, and it seemed to get stronger with each step. Rather than weave through the activity on the wharf, I glided down Pickford Way for a shortcut to the lighthouse. A light green Volkswagen Bug, a cute one with a soft top, was parked right in front of the path leading out to the point where the Pickford Lighthouse, with its squat black hat and big yellow light, loomed over a jagged cliff of rocks. Marty was next to the cute, little keeper's house with its powder white siding and brick red roof shingles. A young woman stood nearby leaning down to a camera that was propped up on a tripod. Marty was wearing a nice gray sweater, blue scarf and a proud grin as the woman took his picture next to his lighthouse.

I stood out of the way and watched as she snapped a few more shots. A sharp gust of air that could definitely be categorized as wind shot across the point causing the woman to straighten from the camera. She reached into her faded jeans and pulled out a hair band to tie back her curly, strawberry blonde hair. She began to readjust her tripod. With his photo session paused, Marty took the time to wave to me.

I decided it was invitation enough to talk to him. I walked toward Marty.

Marty Tate had the kindest gray eyes, like smoke curling up from a cozy fire. "Lacey Pinkerton, I haven't seen you around for a bit." His voice was a little more creaky than the last time we spoke, but he was just as lively as ever. He waved his arm around. "Can you believe this? The Pickford Lighthouse is going to be in a book."

"Really? How exciting, and well deserved, I might add. There is no finer lighthouse on this coast."

Marty beamed at the compliment. "I have to agree. By the way, this is Heather Houston, the talented photographer who is creating a book totally dedicated to lighthouses."

"Nice to meet you. I'm Lacey, town florist and ardent fan of Marty and his tall lady here."

Heather pushed forward her hand. "She is a beauty and Marty is pretty great too." Heather was twenty-something with round blue eyes and the kind of looks that suited life on a California beach. She also had to deal with the same hair issues as me. The next burst of wind sent our curls into a frenzy. I pushed mine behind my ears, and she tightened the band she had just tied into her hair.

She looked out toward the water. "Seems like the wind is really kicking up. I'd like to try for a few more shots, Marty, before we wrap up for the day."

"I'm not going anywhere and neither is my tall lady." Marty winked at me.

"I'll get out of your way," I said. "Marty, I just dropped by to ask you a few questions about your mom, if you don't mind. I had two customers this morning. I believe one was an old friend of yours, Mary Russel?" I ended in a question to see if the name rang a bell. It did.

He chuckled. "Mary and I used to play hopscotch right there on that pathway." He pointed to the cement path I'd just walked. "I suppose she's getting flowers for her birthday party. Just got my invite in the mail."

"Yes, her daughter ordered some lilac centerpieces." The photographer seemed to be ready for the next shot, so I had to move along my request. "Do you think we could meet this evening? I want to ask you a few questions."

Perfectly charming laugh lines crinkled around his eyes when he smiled. "You're still trying to solve that Hawksworth murder, eh? James mentioned you were hot on the trail."

"A murder?" Heather said, sounding slightly stunned. "In this quiet town? I find it hard to believe."

Marty chuckled. "Lacey, here, is quite the detective. She has helped solve quite a few murders. And, yes, it's a quiet town, but you know sometimes it's those quiet ones that have the most secrets." He winked at me again, although this time I wasn't exactly sure why.

Heather seemed somewhat stunned. I wasn't sure if she found it hard to believe that I'd helped solved murders or that there were actual murders in Port Danby, but I decided to turn the conversation away from death.

"What kind of book will this be? A travel guide?" I asked.

"Huh? Oh, yes, the book." She was slightly flustered. I wondered if she would add a mention of Port Danby's propensity for murder under the photos of our lighthouse. That might not be good for tourism or business. Then I quickly reminded myself that our main point of interest was the Hawksworth mansion precisely because it was the site of a grisly family murder.

Heather adjusted the lens on her camera. "It will be one of those coffee table books," she continued. "Lots of glossy photos and descriptions. Now, Mr. Tate, if I could get you to move just a little to your right." She motioned with her hand to direct him.

I stood back and watched as Marty grinned for the camera. The camera clicked just as a brisk gust ruffled Marty's thin white hair. He reached up to smooth it down. "Sorry," he said. "My hair doesn't want to cooperate in this wind."

Another gust pushed against all of us causing Marty to lose balance and take a side step. His laugh was deep and a touch hoarse. "Seems like mother nature is not going to cooperate either."

A low, fluffy line of gray clouds had gathered far out on the horizon. "Looks like we might get a bit of weather," he continued.

The next gust sprayed us lightly with sand from the beach. Instinctively, I shaded my eyes and turned from the onslaught.

Heather snatched her camera off the tripod. "I agree. The weather is not cooperating."

Marty pointed with a gnarled finger toward Heather's black leather camera bag. "You should pack that camera away, or you'll end up with sand in the lens. It's spraying pretty good now."

Heather hung the camera around her neck. "No, it'll be fine. I guess we should continue this tomorrow. Will noon work for you?"

"Sure thing," Marty answered. He smiled my direction. "And you and I have a date this evening. How about seven?"

"Seven is perfect," I said. "I'll bring one of Elsie's lemon and poppy seed pound cakes."

"Oh, that Elsie." He turned to Heather. "If you haven't stopped by the Sugar and Spice Bakery yet be sure to make time for some of Elsie's treats. They are superb." He sent his crinkly smile my direction again. "Lemon and poppy sounds good. I'll put on a pot of coffee and pull out some old photographs. They might be of use in your investigation." Another wink. I really couldn't get enough of Marty's winks. They were adorable.

"Nice meeting you, Heather. By the way, is that your Volkswagen?" I asked as I headed back toward Pickford Way.

"Yes it is. I've had it forever. Nice meeting you too and good luck with your investigation," she called.

I pulled my coat collar up around my ears to protect them from the cold wind and hurried my pace to get back to the warmth of the shop.

CHAPTER 6

$\mathcal{I}$t was an hour until closing. Ryder was sweeping up debris from around the potting station, and I had finished with my dull paperwork for the day. I had texted Elsie to put aside a poppy and lemon pound cake for my visit with Marty. I couldn't wait to see the photographs of the early days in Port Danby. With any luck, I'd uncover more clues in the Hawksworth mystery, but even if that wasn't the case, it would still be fun to listen to Marty's tales about the past.

I headed out of the office and plucked my coat off the hook. The rowdy breeze had pushed the offshore clouds over the town, and the temperature had dropped a good ten degrees.

"Ryder, I'm just heading over to Elsie's to pick up my lemon pound cake before she leaves for the day."

"All right," he called as I walked out.

Elsie was just finishing putting the final gleam on her already spotless glass cases when I walked inside. One lone pink bakery box sat atop the counter.

Elsie glanced over her shoulder but kept shining the glass. "I was just about to drop that off. I've got to head home and help Britney pack." She lowered her cloth. "I'm happy she got this internship. It'll be a big boost for her career. On the other hand, I'm back to square one. No one to assist me in the bakery. Although, I'm also glad she's getting away from Dash. Her head was always in the clouds when it came to that man." She added an aggravated head shake.

"Well, just between you and I, I think *that man* is hurting about this whole thing."

Elsie put her hands on her hips. "Do you mean to tell me after all this acting aloof and indifferent, Dash is actually heartbroken? Good," she said, before I could respond. "But I won't tell Britney. She's liable to change her mind and give up this great opportunity."

I picked up the bakery box. "Hmm, smells good and citrusy. Put it on my tab, will ya?" I laughed. "Boy, if that doesn't just spell out everything about me, a woman with a bakery tab. Guess it's better than a bar tab. Maybe."

"Are you having a romantic dinner with James?" Elsie asked as she finished her polishing task.

"Nope. Marty Tate."

Her face popped up. "So you've tossed aside the handsome Detective Briggs, the town's most eligible bachelor, for the century old lighthouse keeper?" She shrugged. "Marty does have that charismatic smile."

"Doesn't he? I'm hoping he has some pieces to add to my Hawksworth puzzle." I headed toward the door.

"Oh wait, I nearly forgot. I need my taste testers to give my new chocolates a try. I'm making them for the holidays, that is, if you and the other notorious sweet tooth across the street approve." She motioned toward Lola's Antiques.

I feigned a teenage sounding groan. "If we have to. You know how I hate these taste testing chores."

"Well, I could get—"

"Oh my gosh, total sarcasm, woman."

"I know. Just wanted to see how you reacted." She flicked her dusting cloth at me like a guy's locker room towel smack. "I'll get them. They taste like caramel, but they don't contain butter or sugar."

27

"Is that a nod toward Lester? He looks good, by the way. The dictator sister diet, as he calls it, has been working."

"Yep, he's lost about ten pounds since his last doctor's visit." She disappeared into her kitchen and walked out with a cellophane wrapped plate, cold from the refrigerator. Six perfectly round chocolate coated balls were covered with various toppings like crushed nuts and coconut flakes.

I saluted her before taking the candy dish. "I will fulfill all my duties as a taste tester and report back soon." Taking my task very seriously, I headed straight across to Lola's. Mostly, I worried that if I didn't take half of the chocolates directly to Lola, I risked eating them all myself.

Lola's red hair was all I spotted behind the front counter. She popped up to see who had entered. "Oh, it's you."

"Yes, happy to see you too, best friend. And here I made the journey across Harbor Lane to bring you chocolate treats from Elsie."

"Yummy. Perfect timing." She reached under the cellophane for a nut covered chocolate. "I had lunch too early today, and I was starting to really slide into a low blood sugar slump."

I plucked out a coconut covered treat, and the two of us moaned in unladylike fashion as we nibbled the decadent, gooey treats.

"Wow, that magical baker has done it again," Lola cooed. "There must be a pound of butter in this one tiny ball. How does she condense all that buttery goodness into one chocolate coated ball?"

I smiled, pleased to provide Lola with a surprising fact about the confection she had just pushed into her mouth. "No butter or sugar," I said succinctly. "She doesn't want to spoil Les's diet."

Lola shook her head emphatically and reached for another. "Impossible. This tastes like caramel."

I held up two fingers. "Scout's honor." I grabbed out a pistachio covered chocolate. The front door opened as we both commenced with the second part of the taste test. I pointed out a bit of chocolate on her lip before she rounded the counter to help the customer.

"How can I help you?" she asked.

"I'm looking for a vintage necklace," the deep voice responded.

I finished gobbling up the second chocolate and spun around to see who was attached to the nice baritone voice. It took me only a second to realize I'd seen the man before. Even though I'd only seen him on a small phone screen, I was sure the tall, fit and perfectly postured man standing in Lola's shop was Kate's new boyfriend. He never came in to buy flowers, as Kate had anticipated. Indeed, it seemed he had decided on something far more shiny and lasting than roses. I pretended to be interested in a set of porcelain dishes on an oak antique Hoosier cabinet while surreptitiously continuing my survey of the man.

Lola led him over to the glass cabinet that contained all the vintage jewelry. Lola had some truly dreamy pieces with pink pearls, silver woven like lace and pendants that sparkled with color.

Lionel, an unusual name that was easy to remember, leaned into the cabinet to peruse the necklaces. Lola was holding back a pleased smile. Generally, the antique jewelry, especially pieces made with real silver, gold and gemstones, went for a pretty price. It seemed Kate hadn't been overzealous when she bragged that her new boyfriend was rich. She hadn't been dating him long, but it seemed he was already buying her something extravagant. There would be no living with the woman, but I hoped, this time, she had found her true match.

Lionel was sporting slightly grayed temples, a requirement for older rich men, apparently. His sweater and well-pressed slacks fit his impressive physique perfectly as if they had been custom made or, at the very least, fitted at an expensive department store.

A sneeze threatened and I rubbed my nose to push away the tickle. It seemed Lionel liked to wear a great deal of cologne. It had taken a few seconds to circle the various pieces of furniture and waft my direction, but now, it was overwhelming my sensitive, little snout. Boomer lifted his drowsy head from his pillow and released a sneeze of his own.

"Bless you," I said without thinking.

Lionel and Lola looked my direction. I picked up a pale blue teacup. "I think I'll probably end up with this one. It'll match my—my tea set, which is blue." I forced a smile. Lola stared at me past her customer's shoulder as if I'd just lost my mind, but being my best friend, who knew me quite well, she immediately deduced that something was up and that it had to do with her distinguished looking customer.

I continued to show great interest in the porcelain tea cups as Lola found a box for what appeared to be a yellow gold Edwardian style pendant, complete with a tiny diamond and pearl lavaliere. Kate was going to swoon. I wondered how quickly she'd find an excuse to prance into my flower shop to show off her new bauble. I wouldn't blame her. It was beautiful. Although, if I was being totally honest, it seemed a little more suited to an older woman and not young, mod, chic Kate. That might have been the reason for her earlier subdued attire and hairstyle. Maybe she was trying to put on a more conservative, mature woman facade for her new boyfriend.

Lionel's expensive looking watch sparkled as he fished through a series of credit cards looking for a particular one. He pulled it out and handed it over. In the interim, he glanced back over his shoulder and flashed me a brilliant white smile, almost too white.

I returned the smile and fumbled with the tea cups, knocking one off its plate. It clinkered.

"You break it, you buy it," Lola chirped with an impish grin.

I held up the cup. "Not broken."

She handed the box with the necklace to Lionel. He nodded politely to both of us before gliding on expensive loafers to the door. We both stretched our necks to see past Lola's window displays. He climbed into a silver Porsche and drove off. I released the series of sneezes I'd been storing up from the heavy cologne.

"Well, Miss, did you decide which blue teacup would fit with your tea service?" Lola asked when I'd finally stopped sneezing. She yanked a tissue from the box on her counter and handed it to me.

"I was trying to look nonchalant so he wouldn't see me checking him out," I confessed unnecessarily.

"Gathered that, but why? I mean he was nice looking for an old guy. And rich, apparently. That necklace was the most expensive one in the cabinet. Which is why I kept trying my subliminal advertising by touching it and moving it about while he browsed the necklaces. Guess I'm pretty good at the old sleight of hand stuff. Geez, you're not thinking of giving that gorgeous man of yours the boot to try something more vintage. I mean Porsches are nice but—"

"Oh, would you stop," I said sharply. "Of course I'm not thinking of giving James the boot, and who says *the boot* anymore? That man is Kate's new boyfriend. She came in this morning to brag about him, mostly because Dash was in my shop. But she said he was rich and she mentioned that he'd probably be in to buy her some roses, her favorite. She also admonished me to make a fresh bouquet." I rolled my eyes.

"Kate's new guy, huh? Well, it looks like he decided on jewelry instead of roses," Lola said. "So she's on to the next man already? Hope this one sticks."

"Me too. Somehow, I think she'll be less annoying once she finally gets married." I picked up the last chocolate. (After all, I couldn't leave the job unfinished.)

"Except then she'll be letting us know just how rich she is." Lola picked up her last chocolate.

"What should I tell Elsie?" I asked. "She's waiting to hear from her official taste testers."

"Tell her she should be anointed star baker of the world." She pushed the chocolate between her lips and licked her fingers.

"I will tell her exactly that."

CHAPTER 7

The clouds had brought a distinct gloomy chill to the air, but no rain had fallen. The wind caused the ocean to ripple, frosting the otherwise coal black water with frilly whitecaps that glowed under the moon. Elsie's pound cake was so delightfully dense, the strings on the pink bakery box tightened on my fingers as I carried it with one hand in order to keep my coat collar bunched around my neck with the other. Winter was certainly whispering its arrival on this cold autumn night.

A single yellow porch light showered Marty's tiny front stoop with a warm glow. He'd had such a busy day with the photo session, it wouldn't have surprised me if he'd forgotten about our rather impromptu cake date. I knocked lightly, not wanting to startle him in case he had drowsed off on the sofa or forgotten I was coming.

I was wrong on both accounts. The door swung open and Marty's bright smile greeted me. "Lacey, I was hoping you didn't forget."

"Not a chance." I lifted the box. "I remembered the cake too."

"I put on a pot of coffee." He pointed at the box. "Lemon and poppy?" he asked. I'd worried that he'd forgotten we made plans, and it turned out he even remembered all the details.

"Of course. As soon as I left here, I texted Elsie to put one aside just for us." I stepped into the cozy interior.

Marty carried the box into his kitchen, from which the delicious earthy aroma of hot coffee was billowing. I took off my coat and hung it on an oak and brass coat rack standing near the door. The interior of the house was small and cozy, simply decorated with just the necessities for a comfortable life. Marty's small sofa had a faded spot right next to a side table that held a reading lamp, a book and a pair of metal rimmed glasses. An oil painting of the Pickford Lighthouse hung over a small stone fireplace that was filled with a crackling fire. The heat from the flames was enough to warm the entire room. A round table was set up beneath a picture window that overlooked the ocean. A half finished jigsaw puzzle covered most of the table. I walked over to a set of mahogany shelves that held several more books and an impressive collection of ships in bottles.

I was admiring the details of a miniature reproduction of the U.S.S. *Constitution* when Marty returned with a pewter serving tray. He had sliced off two slabs of the pound cake and placed them on white china plates. The coffee splashed about in two porcelain cups as he lowered the tray to a cherry wood coffee table in front of the sofa.

"That one is my favorite," Marty said.

I looked back at him, slightly confused.

He walked over to the bottle collection and picked up the one I'd been admiring. "Old Ironsides, that was what they called her back in her glory day. Bill, an old friend of mine, made all these. He's long since gone, like most of my friends," he said with just enough sorrow it made my throat bunch up. "That's the one big drawback of living to a very old age," he said. "You have to bear losing everyone you knew and loved." After a wistful moment, his smile returned. "Shall we have some cake?"

"Absolutely."

I sat down but Marty shuffled around the end of the couch. "I pulled out my mother's box of photographs." He reached down and picked up a small wooden box that had a lighthouse carved on the side. The paint had long since worn off.

I rose from the sofa cushion. "Can I help you with that?"

"No, no, you sit down and have your cake. I've got it. It's not too heavy," he said with a grunt as he lowered it onto the table next to the pewter tray. "Considering how cumbersome and inconvenient photography was back in my mother's day, there is quite a nice collection. She tended to label names on the back of the photos as well." He reached for a piece of cake. "Was there something in particular you were looking for?"

"Not something," I said between bites. "Someone."

Marty paused our conversation long enough to enjoy the bite of rich, lemony cake. He shook his head. "God bless Elsie and her baking talents."

"Amen," I said and took another bite.

Marty set his plate down and flicked open the tiny brass latch on the box. Its hinges creaked as he lifted the lid. I could almost smell the years, the joys, the sadness, the events that made up a family's long life.

Marty glanced over at his jigsaw puzzle table. "Now, where did I put those glasses?"

I put my plate down. "They are right here on the side table." I swiveled around and picked them up.

"Thank you." Marty's fingers had a slight tremble as he pulled on the glasses. The lenses made his soft gray eyes giant. He turned back to his mother's wooden chest of photographs. He fingered through a few, then pulled out one that was covered with a thin sheet of paper. He lifted the paper back to expose a picture of an attractive woman with dark wavy hair and an almost mischievous smile. I was no expert but it seemed she was wearing a Victorian era wedding dress.

Marty stared at the picture with admiration. "This was my mother, Elizabeth, on her wedding day. It was taken in 1880. This is a daguerreotype. Still looks good, doesn't it?"

"Like it was taken yesterday."

Marty chuckled. "Well, that might be pushing it."

"Maybe. She is lovely, Marty. And I must say, she looks as if she was quite the character. Most of the women in Victorian era pictures look so stern. Did she have a good sense of humor?"

"That she did. You're very perceptive." He lowered the protective sheet of tissue over his mother's photograph and reached into the box for another stack that was folded between some brown paper. "I have them organized by type of photos. These brown, blurry photos are all salt prints. Mid nineteenth century photographers used sodium chloride, better known as salt, to make the photos more light sensitive. This is a picture of what we now call Harbor Lane."

I pulled out my own glasses so I could get a good look at the picture. The police station was a square cement building with only one small window. The place where Franki's Diner now stood was merely a green space filled with a few carts from local fishermen selling the day's catch. One woman in a gray shawl and long layers of skirts held out a bouquet of flowers. There was a wagon filled with flowers next to her, and several women were looking over the blooms.

I pointed at the photo. "This woman was my predecessor. The first Port Danby florist."

Marty chuckled. "I suppose so. I wasn't born yet, so I don't remember this little open market area. Once the Hawksworth shipyard project was stopped, the town built the wharf. That way, fishermen could sell their catch right off the boats. I remember my mother would hand me a dime and say, 'Marty, go buy a nice piece of fish. Smell it first to make sure it's fresh.'"

"Good advice," I said.

"I guess your nose would smell a bad fish from a mile away," he added.

"I can smell a good one from that far too. I think that's why I rarely eat seafood. Just a bit too odorous for me." I scrutinized the photo more. "It looks as if the photographer was standing right about where Lola's Antiques is now. Harbor Lane was just a wide dirt road. There aren't any shops except for this barber shop. It seems to be sharing space with a fishing tackle shop. I don't even recognize that building." I looked up at Marty.

"No, I still remember when they knocked those old buildings

down to put up some more modern shops. My friends and I stood all day on the side of the road watching as big men took sledgehammers to everything. Then they piled all the debris onto carts and dragged it away. The street was paved once horse carriages were replaced with motorcars. I think it was Fielding Price, our current mayor's grandfather, who decided to name it Harbor Lane. Not terribly original but then the Prices were never known for finesse."

"Our current mayor sure doesn't like me," I said. "I'm not quite sure what I did to get him in such a ruffle, other than that I was new to town and I had an unusual pet bird. I did somehow ruffle him more by asking him about a distant relative, Jane Price." I shifted on my seat to face him more. "Actually, Jane Price was the main reason for me to come here."

He pressed his hand to his chest. "Now I'm heartbroken. I thought you just wanted to spend some time sharing a piece of cake with ole Marty." He grinned afterward to assure me he was teasing.

"Well, if it helps, I am enjoying this little cake party immensely. Thank you for letting me take up your evening."

Marty placed his hand over mine. "The pleasure is all mine."

CHAPTER 8

$\mathcal{T}$ ime had swept by as Marty told me stories about Port Danby. I could have listened to him all night.

"Should we have one more slice of cake before looking at more pictures?" he asked.

I patted my stomach. "I think I've had my limit, but please, don't let me stop you."

Marty put his glasses back on and adjusted them on his nose. "No, I think I've reached my limit as well." He leaned into the box. "Ah ha, here is a picture of my mother and father standing with Mayor Harvard Price."

I instantly recognized the rotund man with the imperial chin lift. "When did your father die? You haven't talked much about him."

Marty's gaze dropped behind his glasses. "Yes, my father died when I was just seven. His fishing boat got caught in a squall, and the vessel sank, taking my father with it."

"Oh, I'm sorry to hear that. You were so young. It's good you had such a marvelous, energetic mother."

His smile returned but it was still edged with sadness. It was so long ago, but I was sure he still remembered every detail of that terrible day as if it were yesterday. "My mother was energetic and she had to be. I was quite the handful. But we managed, the two of us." He looked at the picture again. "My mother never liked Harvard Price. She didn't mind his son, Fielding though. I think Harlan takes after his great granddad. So don't take it too personally if the mayor is unfriendly toward you. If you ask me, that Harlan Price is just a grumpy old man. Never could figure out how he got himself elected. He lacks even an ounce of charisma."

I picked up the cup of coffee. It was good and warm on such a chilly night. "Well, from what I've read in my research, the Port Danby mayor position is all part of a family legacy."

"That's true. Harvard Price cemented himself into the position and from there passed the mayoral keys on to his kin. Just like a royal family, I suppose."

The mention of Harvard Price focused me back on my main quest. "Mary Russel mentioned that your mother was very social and that she knew everyone in town."

My comment produced a proud grin. "Indeed, she had so many friends, this house would be filled with people on Sunday afternoon after church. Everyone would stop by with pies and biscuits just to have tea with my mother. She was quite the advice giver, apparently." He laughed. "Not sure if it was always good advice but I suppose there must have been some merit to it if people were willing to hand over perfectly good pumpkin and apple pies."

"I would say so. And if they kept coming back, she must have been handing out solid advice. Was it about marriage issues or health or keeping house?"

"Everything. You name it. I still remember one woman, Mabel was her name. Kept coming back with this terrible toothache and, naturally, my mother was not a dentist. Although, dentistry was nothing short of torture back then with rusty implements and nothing to dull the pain except strong whiskey. My poor mother kept telling her she should go to see the dentist over in Mayfield, but the woman had no money and she was afraid of what he might do. So my mother had the woman sit in one of her kitchen chairs and lean her head back. I was eight years old at the time and curious as heck about what my mother planned to do for poor Mabel. Mother held a gas lantern over the woman's face and stared through a magnifying glass into her mouth." A low chuckle rolled up from his chest as he transported himself back in time. "My mother placed the lantern confidently on the kitchen table and said, 'Mabel, I've got just the thing for you.' Then, with the same confidence, Mother was brimming with it, she marched over to the cupboard where she would store a few treats. She always kept them up too high for me to reach without pulling a chair across the floor." Marty's gray brows danced a little. "Tried that once and couldn't sit down for a week. Anyhow, she dragged over a chair, climbed up and pulled down the tin of salt water taffy she'd made a few weeks earlier for the town fair. She handed Mabel a big lump of the vanilla taffy and told her to chew it on the left side of her mouth, the side with the bad tooth." Marty sat back with a laugh. "I can still remember Mabel's expression." He lifted his fingers and curled them around his eyes like fake glasses. "Eyes as big as saucers. I think she was having second thoughts about relying on my mother for her dental needs. Mother stood there with fists on her hips waiting for Mabel to follow her instructions."

"Did she?" I asked, anxious to hear how the unorthodox dentistry worked.

"She did. Shoved that whole piece in so that the whole left side of her face looked as if she was a chipmunk storing nuts. Her eyes scrunched up in pain." Marty put on a good visual of Mabel trying to eat taffy with a bad tooth. "She chewed and chewed. Then her eyes popped open, and she smiled around that mouthful of candy. Mother knew just what to do. She pulled the wastebasket out from the kitchen pantry and held it out. Mabel spit out the rest of the taffy and the bad tooth came with it. After that, she brought mother and me her special molasses cookies every week for a month."

"Sounds like a nice payment. What a great story. Marty, do you know if your mom knew Jane Price? She was Harvard's daughter from his first marriage. I think she might have been a town treasurer or accountant at some point in time."

Marty tapped his chin. "Jane Price. Jane Price," he repeated. Then his brows hopped up. "You know, I think I've seen her name on one of these old pictures." He hunched over to dig in the box, and I tried to keep from springing off the couch and doing a little happy dance.

"Hmm, let me see," he muttered into the hollow box. "I think it was one of these newer albumen prints." He paused long enough to turn his head over his shoulder. "Can you believe they actually used egg whites to get a clearer picture that wouldn't fade. It worked, too." He turned back into the box. "Yes, let me see." He lifted out a picture. "This is it." He turned it over to read the back. "Yes, Jane Price 1902. I never met her." He handed me the picture. "My mother is on the right. Jane is the one holding flowers."

I brought the picture closer. "Yes, this is her. I've seen a picture of her in a newspaper. She was standing behind her father's desk. From what I read in my research, she left town a few years after this picture was taken."

"Occasionally, my mother and I would take this old box out and go through the collection of photos. I remember asking her about the lady in the picture, Jane Price. She said they were friends and that Jane was the mayor's daughter. She never said why Jane left town though. Of course, I probably never asked."

I stared at the photo a long time, trying to catch all the details, trying to get a sense of the woman and then it occurred to me, the most important detail was staring me right in the face. "She's holding a bouquet of lavender," I said.

Marty looked over at the picture. "Yes, I think my mother told me she used to grow lavender in the field behind the mayor's office. She used it in soap and cooking."

"Interesting," I said as I sat back somewhat flabbergasted. Had I just landed on something big?

"Why is that so interesting? I believe lavender is still used for those same purposes today."

I sat forward again, still clutching the picture. "I should explain. In my research, I've gone through the old trunk in the gardener's shed up at the house."

Marty's forehead crinkled. "Did you now? I thought the trunk was locked."

I smiled coyly. "It was but I found the key. It is filled with Bertram Hawksworth's belongings, including a few love letters from someone called Button. One of the letters had a dried sprig of lavender inside it. It had been preserved there all these years."

"Do you think Jane might have written the letters to Bertram? Maybe the whole thing was a crime of passion." Marty poured another cup of coffee and stirred in some sugar. "Of course, lavender has always grown abundantly in this area."

"I'm sure and it's a commonly used dried flower." The fire had dwindled during our long chat, and without thinking, I rubbed my arms for warmth.

"You're cold. I'll put another log on the fire." Marty, gentleman that he was, hopped up from the couch. (Amazingly well for someone his age. Heck, amazingly well for someone my age.)

"I think I've taken up enough of your time tonight, Marty. I should be on my way." I stood up and leaned over to pick up the pewter tray.

"Oh no, you can just leave that, Lacey. I'll take care of it in the morning." He patted his hand over his mouth to stifle a yawn. "I guess it is rather late. I could reminisce about the past all night long, especially with such an appreciative audience. I must say, most people, particularly young people like yourself, aren't interested in past events and historical details."

I reached for my coat. "I've always loved it. How else can you know anything about the future if you're not tuned in to the past?"

Marty beamed. "I knew I liked you the moment we met." He squinted one eye. "It was on the holiday horse and carriage ride, wasn't it?"

"You remember." I relaxed my shoulders. "Of course you do. Your memory is incredible."

His gray eyes twinkled. "You mean for someone my age."

"No, I mean in general. I wish I had it." I pulled on the coat.

"Well, I have less going on in my life. You're a successful business owner with lots of things going on in that pretty head. Most of my time is spent with my books or puzzles and the tall lady standing next to this house. I liked that you referred to the lighthouse as my tall lady. I know it sounds odd, but I do sometimes feel an extraordinary connection to the lighthouse."

I walked over, hopped on my toes and kissed his cheek. "There is nothing odd about that at all because she *is* extraordinary."

"I see you appreciate that old tower as much as me." He walked me to the door. "I'm sorry I couldn't be of any more help in your investigation."

I turned to him before walking out. "Are you kidding? This was one of my best research sessions ever. Like you said, maybe it was a crime of passion. That idea intrigues me so much, I'll probably have a tough time sleeping tonight with all the possible theories bouncing around my head."

"Well then, I apologize in advance for your soon to be restless night."

I stepped out on the stoop. "Let's do this again, Marty."

"I would really enjoy that, Lacey. Good night."

CHAPTER 9

$\mathcal{J}$t had been a hectic morning with mostly single purchase customers. No big orders. Sometimes I preferred just the occasional bouquet request to large wedding orders. Way less pressure and stress. Unfortunately, the single bouquet purchases would never be enough to keep me in business. It was the big event orders that made Pink's Flowers a success.

Elsie texted to see what Lola and I thought of the chocolates. I decided to walk over and tell her firsthand that we gobbled them with unladylike speed and fervor. Ryder was glancing through a catalog of vases and pots.

"I'm just going to stop next door to talk to Elsie. Text if we get a sudden swarm of customers."

"Sure thing, boss," he said without looking up from his catalog.

Elsie was helping a woman when I walked inside. She peered past the woman's puffed and heavily sprayed silver blonde hair and shot me a wink. I decided to check out all the yummy treats behind the glass while the woman decided which pastries she wanted to add to her dozen. I was admiring a tray of tiny tarts, each decorated with little candy flowers, when a flash of sparkle caught my eye. Elsie's customer was wearing a beautiful gold necklace, and it looked very familiar.

The customer, a nicely dressed woman of sixty plus, caught me admiring the necklace. She fingered the pearl and smiled proudly.

"I'm sorry," I said, "can I get a better look? It's so unique."

The woman turned to me and lifted her chin, so I could see the entire necklace. I was definitely looking at the vintage jewelry Lionel had purchased from Lola the day before.

"It's lovely," I said. "Do you know what year it was made?" I decided to pry, hoping to get a little information out of her.

"I believe it's Edwardian. Real gold, of course. It was a gift," she added with a simpering smile.

It seemed Kate was not going to be getting a necklace, after all. It was easy to deduce that the woman was somehow related to Lionel, an aunt, perhaps.

"It's stunning, isn't it?" Elsie said. "I was admiring it before you came in." She finished tying the string on the bakery box and handed it to the woman. "Here you go, Margaret. I hope your book club enjoys them."

"I'm sure they will, Elsie. See you in two weeks." She nodded politely at me and carried her pastries out the door.

I watched through the window as she climbed into a Cadillac and drove away. I turned back to Elsie. "Who is she?" I asked.

"That's Margaret Sherwood. She lives in one of those big houses in Chesterton. A very wealthy widow. Her husband left her a fortune. I think he was in cargo shipping or something like that. She comes in here every other week to buy pastries for her book club."

"I saw a man buy that necklace from Lola yesterday," I said. "That's why it caught my eye. She must be a relative or something."

"Not a relative." Elsie walked over to a tray of chocolate chip cookies, picked one up and handed it to me. We were at that point in our friendship where she no longer needed to ask. She always just assumed that I required some sort of sugary treat when I entered her shop. I always felt a little guilty that I didn't have an easy to hand out goodie when she came to my shop, but handing her a single carnation or rose was hardly the equivalent of one of her delicious cookies.

Elsie wore a lopsided grin. "Apparently, after five years of widowhood, Margaret has found herself a new boyfriend."

A cookie crumb sucked into my throat at the word boyfriend. I covered my mouth to cough it free.

"Should I get you some water?" Elsie asked during my cough fit.

I nodded and she raced to the kitchen and returned with a glass of water. I was catching my breath and wiping the tears from my eyes as she handed it to me. I took a few good gulps, then sighed with relief. "Thanks."

"Since I know this isn't your first time eating a cookie," Elsie quipped, "I can only assume my statement about Margaret finding a boyfriend caused that crumb to take a wrong turn."

I nodded and swallowed again to make sure everything was clear of cookie. "Yes, I was sure she was just an elderly relative."

"Elderly?" Elsie asked. "How did you know he was younger? Margaret, of course, made a point of bringing up his age, forty-two apparently. He's a good twenty years younger than her. And rich too, it seems. He just moved into the house next to hers, a big Colonial that's been vacant for years. She says he's quite handsome, only I'm picturing a forty-year-old with thinning hair, a double chin and a belly that hangs below his belt."

I shook my head. "You'd be wrong," I said smugly and took a more cautious bite.

"So, he's not hairless with multiple chins?" Elsie picked up the tray of cookies and carried them to a silver platter. She began placing them in a neat array on the platter for display in her glass cabinet.

"He's tall, very fit and has just a touch of gray at the temples. Definitely handsome."

Elsie lowered the last cookie to the tray as she peered up at me. "You've got to be kidding? Well, good for Margaret. She's a nice person, and it has taken her a long time to get over the heartbreak of losing her husband. She seems very happy."

I finished the cookie without another choking incident. "I don't think this will work out too well for her," I said.

Elsie carried the empty tray to the sink area and walked back out. "Why do you say that?"

"Because the man I saw buy the necklace was the same man Kate showed me on her phone when she was flashing me a picture of *her* new boyfriend, Lionel."

Elsie's eyes popped open wider. "You're kidding? Same guy?"

"I'd bet my flower shop on it. Of course, maybe he has a twin. Although, that seems farfetched."

Elsie sighed. "Poor Kate. She just can't seem to get this whole boyfriend thing right."

"All I know is—if he's dating both women and they live only a few miles apart, that guy is a no good rotten cad." My phone beeped. I pulled it out of my pocket. It was a text from Ryder.

"Looks like we've got a wedding order. Should I get them started with catalogs?"

"Yes please, I'll be right there," I texted back. "I've got to get back to the shop."

"Wait," Elsie said before I could get to the door. "You didn't tell me. How were the chocolates? Were they O.K.?"

I tilted my head in a mocking fashion. "I wonder if Michelangelo asked that about his paintings and sculptures. Hey guys, do you think this perfectly sculpted statue of David is O.K.? Seriously, you are an artist and your goodies are your masterpieces, each one finer and more breathtaking than the next. Including those chocolates."

Elsie held back her grin. "Glad you enjoyed them. What did Lola think?"

I waved my hand. "Oh, she hated them." Her face dropped but only for a second when she realized I was teasing. "Lola said to tell you that you should be anointed star baker of the world. I think we should get that printed on an apron for you with your picture surrounded by stars. By the way, if you weren't using butter or sugar, what made them taste like caramel?"

Elsie coyly touched her chest. "A star baker never shares her baking secrets."

I nodded. "Fine, then I'll assume you're full of baloney and that they are brimming with butter and sugar."

"All right, I'll spill this secret. Dates, they are nature's caramel."

I squeezed my nose up. "Really? Those prune-like sticky things that look like something my grandma would eat for her digestion? Lola is right. You are a magician. And now, I need to sell flowers, so I'll see you later."

"All right and remember to chew your cookies instead of inhaling them," she called as I headed out the door.

CHAPTER 10

*A*fter a great deal of debate and mind changing, my bridal customer had decided on a mix of white roses and orange tulips. It was an unusual mix but one that would go delightfully with her spring themed, early April wedding. I finished filing the order in the folder we had started for next year's events. I thumbed through the other orders. "Wow, I just added April." I looked up at Ryder who was cleaning the windows. "That means we already have at least one huge event for the first four months of the new year, and we haven't even passed Thanksgiving yet. That's pretty darn cool. It also means that you won't ever be able to leave here to go on your horticulture adventure."

Ryder moved his arm in circles around the glass. "I don't know about that. After that last nice raise you gave me, I'll be reaching my goal faster than I thought."

"Then I should withdraw it. I'll never be able to replace you. I guess I'll just shut down when you leave." I pulled out Kingston's treat can, which immediately woke him from a long afternoon nap. He started his glide back and forth across his perch as he eagerly waited for one of the peanut butter dog treats Elsie created for the bakery. They were Kingston's favorite. I walked over to his perch and stared absently out the window as Kingston yanked the treat from my fingers.

I joked with Ryder but the truth was I was terrified at the prospect of him leaving. It would be impossible to fill his shoes, and he had become such a good friend. His leaving would definitely leave a void in all our lives. And, in particular, a certain best friend, who I suddenly spotted, sporting her dark green fedora and a Led Zeppelin t-shirt as she walked quickly across Harbor Lane. Ryder noticed her too.

"Uh oh," he said, "she looks upset." He stopped his task and lifted his eyes in thought, then shook his head. "Nope, can't think of anything I did today to upset her but then you never know with Lola."

The bell rang and Lola walked inside. "Oh my gosh, do I have a big mouth." She stopped and pointed at her mouth. "Do you see this hole? It's way too big and sometimes stuff just flows out of it and then I have to insert my foot to stop the flow." She released a sort of half sigh and half groan. "I need a hug." She flicked her gaze my direction. "No offense but I think I'll fill that need over there with the tall, good looking window cleaner."

"No offense taken," I said.

Lola tromped across the shop, and Ryder obliged her with a long hug and a light kiss.

"Thanks, hunky window cleaner, I needed that, and by the way, since you've got all the tools needed, that shop across the street could use a little window cleaning too."

"You gonna pay me?" Ryder asked with a teasing smile.

"Oh, you'll be handsomely rewarded," Lola answered back with a flirty run of her fingers up his arm.

"All right, well, I've witnessed enough of this business transaction," I said. "I've got purchase orders to make."

"Wait." Lola skipped back across to me. "Don't you want to know why I came in here and pointed out my big mouth?"

I blinked at her for a few seconds. "Not sure I want to know. Maybe you should confide in your window washer."

"No, I think this will be far more interesting to the bird feeder."

She took a second to walk over and favor Kingston with a nice head rub. He was so thrilled to have the attention of his first and only crush, he nearly dropped the last bits of his peanut butter treat.

"How did your big mouth get you in trouble today?" I asked.

"It was all very innocent on my part. I mean, how was I to know that Kate's new boyfriend bought a necklace for another woman? I thought she was a relative or something."

I stood up straighter. "That's the first thing I thought too. I saw a woman wearing the necklace when I went to the bakery. But she told Elsie it was a gift from her new boyfriend."

Lola stopped rubbing Kingston's head, but he kept his eyes glued to her. "I just assumed Margaret was his aunt. I mean she's so much older. Margaret is an elderly widow. She comes to the antique shop occasionally to look for trinkets." Lola rubbed her fingers together. "Big bucks too."

"Yes, I heard all that from Elsie. All right, this is getting sort of confusing. Tell me from the start what happened." We moved our conversation over to the stools. Kingston flew over to the work island to join us, or Lola, more likely.

"So I had lunch. I made myself the best hummus filled flatbread thing with tomatoes and cucumbers and—" She waved her hand. "Never mind, I'll tell you about it later."

"Good idea. So when did you see Kate?"

"Well, that was why I brought up the lunch. I was nibbling on a piece of cucumber, thumbing through a magazine, when the shop bell rang. Kate entered, looking very serious, like a girl on a mission. By the way, not loving her new old fashioned prude look. What's with the pale blue sweater and pressed pants? And her hair looked like something I'd see my Aunt Sally wear to a church social."

I sighed loudly. "Focus, lady. And yes, I agree, her new style doesn't suit her at all, but I think she's dressing that way because of her new boyfriend."

Lola laughed dryly. "Not anymore. Good ole big mouth." She pointed at herself. "I put a quick end to her fairy tale romance with the rich guy."

"What did you do?" I asked. "And how on earth did you get involved in the first place?"

"You know, lucky me. I always manage to step into trouble, even when it's not looking for me."

Ryder laughed quietly and quickly stifled it.

"I heard that, handsome window washer. Just for that, you can clean all the windows in my house too." Lola turned back to me. "Kate came up while I was swallowing my cucumber, and she looked quite anxious about something. She told me she'd spotted her new boyfriend going into the antique shop, and she was wondering what he was shopping for. Well, I knew exactly who she was talking about because you mentioned it to me when you brought me those dazzling little chocolate thingamabobs. I quickly deduced that the man must have been buying the necklace for his aunt or older sister because I saw Margaret wearing the necklace when I was inside Les's coffee shop. Ack! By the way, Les was experimenting with a new gingerbread flavored coffee. I got to taste test it. Yum."

"All right, I'll have to ask Les later why I was not part of that taste test but continue."

"That takes us back to my cucumber. So I'm eating and Kate walks in and wants to know what her new boyfriend was buying in my shop. That's when things got stupid, at least on my part. I told her it was a vintage gold Edwardian necklace, one of the nicest ones in the case and then I continued to tell her—"

I touched her arm. "Oh no, did you tell her that you saw Margaret wearing it?"

"Darn tootin', I did. In my defense, I never considered the possibility that Margaret was seeing Lionel. She must be a good twenty years older."

"What happened after that?" I asked.

"It looked as if Kate was about to shoot flames from her ears, so I quickly suggested that Margaret might be an aunt or dear old friend but Kate wasn't buying it. She said Lionel was new in town, and he never mentioned any family or friends. Then she swung around on her sensible shoes and marched out the door. So, there you have my

51

first major fumble of the day, and it's still early. Who knows what other catastrophic damage I could cause with my overlarge mouth?"

I hopped off the stool and Lola followed. "Don't be too hard on yourself. I assumed the same thing about Margaret. It seems Kate has picked another winner. That poor woman. I wonder how she keeps getting this so wrong?"

Lola sashayed over to Ryder for another quick kiss. She smiled back at me over her shoulder. "We can't all be masters at picking men, can we?"

"So true."

CHAPTER 11

I wrapped my hand around Briggs' arm as we walked out of Franki's Diner. The coastal fog had stayed away, and the dark blue sky was littered with tiny diamonds. A half moon tilted whimsically over the ocean.

"Look at that moon. Isn't it romantic?" I said. "Let's take a walk to the marina."

Briggs glanced up at the sky. Moonlight always looked extra good on him. "I do believe, Miss Pinkerton, that you find every phase of the moon romantic."

I smiled and squeezed his arm tighter. "When I'm with you, Detective Briggs, even the streetlamps are romantic."

We'd just stepped off the curb leaving Franki's parking lot when a woman rushed past us in such a hurry, it took me a few seconds to recognize that it was Heather Houston, the photographer. She had her camera around her neck and was carrying the camera bag as she scurried over the asphalt toward the diner.

"Hello, Miss Houston," I said cheerily.

She startled at the sound of her name. Her face shot my direction. She seemed to be trying to place me but couldn't. "Hello," she said quickly and continued her march toward the diner.

"Not a very friendly person," Briggs noted.

"She definitely seemed distracted." I glanced back. Heather was just entering the diner.

"Who is she?" Briggs asked as we steered our stroll toward the wharf and marina.

"Her name is Heather Houston." I snuggled closer to him for warmth as the coastal chill began to creep toward us. "She is taking photographs for a book about lighthouses. Our town's fair maiden, Pickford Lighthouse, is going to be featured in the book. I met Heather while she was taking pictures of Marty. Oh, that's right, I haven't talked to you since my wonderful evening with Marty."

"That's right. How did that go? Did he have anything interesting to add to your case?" There was a touch of teasing in his tone.

I stopped. "James Briggs, you act as if I'm some silly woman who is delusional in thinking she can solve a murder. I've solved quite a few of them."

He took hold of my hand and pulled me closer for a kiss. "You are so adorable when you are mad." He gazed down at me with those dark brown eyes. The soothing scent that was a mix of his soap and after-shave surrounded me. Any touch of anger vanished.

"And, you don't play fair with that magnetic brown gaze," I complained. "How can a girl stay mad? Although, I'm still sore about your derisive tone when mentioning my case. I'm going to solve it. Just wait and see."

He hugged me. "I have no doubt about it. I'm sorry about teasing you. You're the best assistant a detective could have."

"Partner," I muttered as I peeled myself out of his arms and took hold of his hand to continue our walk.

"Assistant," he muttered in response.

"If you say so," I said, teasingly. "Anyhow, back to marvelous Marty." I laughed at the alliteration. "That's a perfect name for him. He's such a great guy. He told me so many stories that I didn't leave his house until close to eleven."

"Should I be jealous?" he asked.

"Yes, you should. Especially because Marty found an old photograph of his mother standing with her friend Jane Price."

It had been a few months since I'd brought up the Hawksworth investigation so it took Briggs a few seconds to remember the name Jane Price. "Oh, that was Harvard Price's daughter from his first marriage. Do you think she's tied up in all this?"

"Not sure but I think I might be closer to linking her to Bertram Hawksworth."

The wharf was mostly deserted. The shops and kiosks were closed for the night. Without the usual lively conversations, intermittent shrieks of the gulls and rumble of boat motors, our footsteps reverberated on the weathered dock much louder than they would have during a busy day. Aside from the rhythmic thumps and clangs of boats in their slips, the only other sound was a woman's laugh. It rolled out from the boat slips and bounced along planks.

My hand was still wound tightly around Briggs' arm as we trod lightly along the uneven wood planks that made up the long stretch of dock between the moored vessels.

"What did Marty have that is helping you link Jane Price to the Hawksworth murder?" Briggs asked.

"Not sure if I should tell you because you might think I'm just grasping at straws, or, in this case, lavender."

He looked over at me. "Did you just say lavender?"

"Yes. Remember when I told you about the love letters to Teddy from Button? Well, they were in Bertram's trunk with his personal belongings, so it's fairly easy to deduce that he was Teddy. But my intuition tells me that his wife, Jill, was not Button. I think I might have mentioned that there was a piece of dried lavender still stuck inside one of the letters."

"You might have mentioned it," he agreed.

"Well, it just so happens that Jane Price was holding a bouquet of lavender in the picture Marty showed me. He said she used to grow it in a field behind the mayor's office. She made soap out of it."

Briggs tilted his head side to side. "Could mean something or could just be a coincidence."

I was just about to give my view on his comment when a figure climbed out of the boat in the second to last slip of the marina. It was the luxury boat called *Funtasy* where I'd seen the glamorous woman sipping her pink cocktail.

I stopped short, inadvertently pulling Briggs to a stop too. The tall figure leaned down to kiss the aforementioned glamorous woman (only without the pink cocktail) goodbye, then spun on his expensive loafers our direction. The overhead lights on the dock illuminated his face, but I already knew the man leaving the boat was none other than Lionel.

"Boy, that man is busy as a beaver," I muttered under my breath and pulled a confused Briggs along.

Lionel nodded at us. "Evening."

"Evening," Briggs said in return.

I hurried him along, out of ear shot of the boat.

"Why do I get the feeling I'm about to be tied up and thrown onto a pirate boat?" Briggs asked. "Is there a reason you are dragging me toward the end of the marina?"

I turned back to make sure we were far enough away from *Funtasy* and Lionel's other girlfriend.

Briggs was smiling with amusement. "I like it when you get all clandestine, like an adorable secret spy. What is going on?"

"That man we just passed—the one who kissed the woman on that boat goodbye—"

"Yes, I saw all that."

"That is Kate's new, rich boyfriend, the guy who bought the Palmer house." He stared back at me, not quite sure what was stunning enough to cause me to pull him to a quiet place, away from the boats. (Typical man.) His brows rose with sudden comprehension.

"Ah, I see, he was kissing that woman on the boat, and that was definitely not Kate Yardley so he's a two timer."

I held up three fingers. "He's a three timer. Yesterday, he was inside Lola's shop buying an expensive necklace for a widow who lives near him in Chesterton."

"Huh, I don't know whether to be disgusted or impressed," he said off-handedly.

I stared up at him. He caught my scowl.

"Disgusted," he said emphatically. "Definitely disgusted."

"Good answer. Now I'll even invite you to my house for a movie." I took his arm again, and we started the journey back.

CHAPTER 12

he distinctive buzz of a phone woke me from a deep sleep, only as I opened my eyes I realized I wasn't in bed and the pillow under my head was a chest. My arm had fallen asleep, and it tingled as I pushed to sitting. Briggs' head was leaned back against the couch. He was fast asleep, his arm still around me and our legs in somewhat of a tangle. I lowered his arm from around me and rather than wake, he groaned quietly as his head slipped to the side. I fumbled around for the remote and turned off the television.

The phone buzzed again. I tapped his chest. "Hey, sleepy man, that's your phone."

It took him a second to open his eyes. He glanced around confused by his surroundings.

"We fell asleep watching the movie," I explained. "But I think you're needed."

"No, I think *you're* needed." He circled his arms around me and pulled me against him. His phone buzzed again. He groaned louder. He released me and reached for the phone on the coffee table.

"Briggs here." He sat forward. "Go ahead."

I got up to put on some coffee. Something told me he was going to need it. Naturally, I kept a curious ear turned in the direction of the couch.

"Yeah, get the evidence team over there, but tell them not to touch anything until I get there. Text me the address. I'll be there in ten." He got up from the couch, rolled down his shirt sleeves and buttoned the top of his shirt. "Got a dead body over in Chesterton." His phone beeped and he glanced at it. "They just sent me the address. Looks like it's the Palmer house. Maybe that guy cheated on one too many women."

Stunned, I put the coffee pot down. "Is Lionel dead?"

"Not sure yet. They've got a male victim. The neighbors heard a gunshot and decided to call the police." He grabbed his coat from the hook and pulled it on, oblivious to the pleading look I was giving him. He finally noticed it when he walked over to kiss me goodbye.

I stared up at him with my best, pretty please smile.

"It's the middle of the night, Lacey. You don't want to be hanging out at a murder scene at this hour."

I switched to my annoyed brow raise look.

He stared down at me. "Oh, all right, get your coat."

I did the fast clap and tap shoe dance, then hurried to the coat hook. "Good thing we fell asleep during the movie. That way we are both rested and ready to investigate."

He helped me put on my coat. "How many people would be this cheery to be woken from a sound sleep and sent out into the cold night air to inspect a corpse?" he asked. "Don't answer that. I already know. One. Just one person in the world." He pulled the hood up on my coat and yanked it down around my ears to draw me closer for a kiss.

We headed out and climbed into his car. He started the motor and turned on the heater. "Did you happen to see the end of the movie?" he asked.

"I think I fell asleep just before the pivotal moment when all was revealed." I pushed the heater vents so they were pointed directly at me.

He backed the car out of the driveway. "Great, so now we'll never know who the murderer was, and I don't think I can sit through the whole thing again just to find out how it ends."

"It was the wife," I said confidently, even though I had no real clue about it. "She had those shifty eyes, and she was wearing tight leather pants. Never trust a woman in tight leather pants."

His wry smile popped up. "Why is that?"

"Can you imagine how uncomfortable tight leather pants would be? You can't be of sound mind if you look in your closet and say, why, I think I'll wear those tight leather pants today. They look super comfy."

Briggs nodded. "Good point. However, it probably wouldn't stand up in court."

The high end Chesterton neighborhood was quiet and dark until we reached the explosion of red flashing lights and police activity at the end of the street. A few neighbors were staring out windows, and some had pulled on plush robes to stand, pale with concern, on their front porches as they watched police and emergency personnel criss-cross the vast front yard of the house that was the center of action. While the other houses on the block had lush, verdant green front lawns, Briggs and I found ourselves hiking over dried, dead weeds. The landscaping was nonexistent in front of the massive home. Lionel's Porsche was sitting in the driveway in front of the garage. The bright light of the evidence team shone through the large front windows of the house.

A policewoman with the Chesterton uniform met us as the front door. She briefly glanced at me before turning her attention back to Briggs. "Sorry to pull you out of bed, Detective Briggs," she started. She gave me a second glance.

"Officer Gillum, this is Lacey Pinkerton—"

"Oh, this is the famous nose," Officer Gillum began then cut herself short. "Sorry, I mean so this is your girlfriend with the million dollar nose." She shook her head. "Sorry again." She nodded at me. "Nice to meet you. I've heard a lot about you and your talents." (I'd only just met her, but I liked her already.)

She led us through the entryway. It became instantly clear that the interior of the house was in need of repair. Shredded strips of pale blue and silver wallpaper curled up along the wainscoting, which was badly in need of sanding and paint. Three electric wires dangled from the ceiling in the spot that probably once held a grand chandelier or light fixture.

"The victim is a male, forty-two, according to his identification. Lionel Dexter," Gillum continued.

It took me a second to absorb the information. It was just yesterday morning when Kate Yardley had been gushing about her new boyfriend. Briggs and I had just seen him kiss a woman on a luxury boat goodbye. And now the man was dead.

"You mentioned the word identification," Briggs said as we were led past two hallways and into a large room with high ceilings and a great view of what I could only assume was Chesterton Bay, only it was too dark to enjoy.

"Yes," Gillum said. "It wasn't a driver's license. Just an Ohio state identification card. We found it in his wallet, which was on the sofa in the sitting room. His credit cards and a hundred dollar bill were still inside. Spoke to a few of the neighbors. Apparently, he only just moved in, which would explain the lack of furniture." She glanced around the large room. It was mostly empty. "I was surprised to hear that someone bought this old wreck."

"I was surprised too," Briggs said.

"Must have gotten a good deal," she said. "I like to watch those restoration projects on the Home and Garden channel, and bringing a big place like this back to its former glory would cost a fortune."

The officers standing around the body parted to allow Briggs and me through. Once again, I was going through some curious scrutiny until Officer Gillum kindly filled them in by pointing to her own nose and winking a few times.

Lionel Dexter was on his back, dressed in a shiny, navy blue silk robe pulled over a pair of pajamas. Blood had spread out from a bullet hole in his chest.

Briggs pulled a pair of latex gloves out of his pocket and handed me a pair as well. The circle of officers seemed to get smaller as they apparently moved in to watch the famous nose in action. I was certainly going to disappoint them. The overwhelming scent of Lionel's expensive cologne hovered in a dense cloud over his body. It would be hard to detect anything else, especially mixed as it was with the pungent smell of blood.

"Cause of death looks pretty obvious," Briggs said. "Has the coroner been called?"

"On their way," Gillum answered.

Briggs peered up at Gillum. "Anything show up in the initial sweep? Any weapon yet?"

"Negative on the weapon," she answered. "The front door was unlocked when we entered. No sign of forced entry so it seems he might have known the killer."

"Officer Gillum," a voice called from the entry. "The coroner's team is here."

"Right, let's clear this area so they can set up," Gillum ordered.

Briggs looked at me. His hair was ruffled from sleep and his shirt was wrinkled, no doubt from me curling against him on the couch. He didn't look his usual polished self. I rather liked the rumpled look. It reminded me of one of those murder shows with the disheveled detective like Columbo. "Do you detect anything unusual, or is his cologne smothering everything else?" He waved his hand in front of his face. "It's a wonder any woman would go near him. He must bathe in the stuff."

"Mariner Number Six," I said, confidently. It had taken me a few whiffs to finally discern which expensive cologne Lionel used, but my time in the perfume industry made me somewhat of an expert on particular brands.

"What is that? Sounds like a code for something." Briggs looked rightly confused. Of course, he had no use for expensive, heavy men's colognes. He made simple soap smell divine.

"That is the name of the cologne he uses—I mean used. I think it costs about a hundred dollars a bottle."

Briggs' brows bunched up. "Seriously? He paid big bucks to smell this pungent?"

"I'm afraid so. It's actually a nice smelling cologne, just not in such a large dose. Apparently, he liked to splash on a lot of it. I noticed it when he walked into Lola's shop to buy the vintage necklace."

"That's right, you have some information about the various women he seemed to be courting. We'll have to talk about that later. Any other smells jump out at you?"

I shook my head. "Nothing I can discern past the cologne and the blood. Not a pleasant mix, I might add."

Voices and activity echoed in the entry, letting us know the coroner's team had arrived.

Briggs offered me his hand and pulled me out of the crouched position. When no one was looking, he discretely reached up and pushed a curl of hair off my face. "Do you want to go back home and climb in bed, or do you want to have a look around the crime scene?" he asked.

"What do you think, Detective Briggs?"

CHAPTER 13

*B*riggs returned to the entry to examine the front door. He ran his gloved hand along the edge of the door and door frame. I ran my sniffer around the room to see if I could catch any lingering scent of perfume but couldn't find even a trace of it. The large house was so empty and with its walls so devoid of wallpaper and proper paint, the porous plaster had absorbed years of mildew and stale air. The entire place should have been fumigated and checked for mold before anyone moved in, but it seemed Lionel Dexter hadn't minded a little stale, sour air.

After a close examination, Briggs shut the door. "Like Gillum noted, no forced entry," he said.

"Makes sense if it was one of his many girlfriends. He would have just invited them in. As long as he wasn't already entertaining," I added wryly.

Briggs nodded. "Maybe he *was* entertaining, and he had an unexpected visitor, exposing his infidelity."

"Possible." I tapped my chin in thought. "Although, the crime scene suggests no struggle, like the killer just walked in and shot her unsuspecting victim point blank as if she had it all planned."

"Good deduction, Miss Pinkerton." We were alone in the entry, so he managed to get in a little squeeze before getting back to business. "I notice you are using the pronoun *she*," he said. "Are you settled on the killer being a woman?"

"I don't know if settled is the right word." We headed back down the hallway toward the kitchen area. "It's just that if the man was seeing various women, then it follows that someone would be left heartbroken, possibly even upset enough to kill."

"Crimes of passion are definitely trending lately. But often the spurned lover goes after the person who has stolen their beloved away from them."

"Yes, that's true, but in this case they went after the beloved. Or maybe it wasn't a crime of passion at all. Rich men tend to have plenty of enemies."

"Good point." Briggs pushed open the door leading into a large kitchen that looked as if it had once been the hub of activity for vast, important social events and holidays. The copper pot and pan rack was still gleaming over a stove that was coated with dust and grease and what could easily be discerned as rat droppings. A dormitory sized refrigerator sat in the nook where a regular sized fridge once sat, according to the warped faded vinyl floor left behind. A long extension cord snaked up from the back of the mini refrigerator, stretching a good ten feet around a very old double oven and a cook's desk, to the nearest outlet.

"Apparently, Lionel's personal chef hadn't arrived yet," Briggs quipped. "So, how do you know the woman on the small yacht?"

"Can *Funtasy* be classified as a yacht?" I asked for no real reason except it was late and my attention was a little scattered. "I wasn't sure whether to consider it a yacht or a luxury cruiser or some such thing. And I don't know the woman Lionel was kissing at the marina."

"If it is way more expensive than any boat I could ever own, I label it a yacht. Of course, that means Bill Trainor's rusty old fishing trawler is a yacht because it's far above my pay grade."

I turned to him. "Are you saying that I should not expect keys to a glamorous yacht under the Christmas tree this year?"

"I could get you the keys and wrap them up in a cute little box if that's what you're hoping for."

I laughed. "Oh my gosh, you can tell the two of us were woken out of a deep sleep just an hour ago."

"True. I suppose we should get back to the murder investigation. It's hard though because my assistant is quite distracting."

"I'll try to distract less."

Briggs headed across the room where a small hallway led to a service porch with a deep sink and wall hooks for coats and hats. I perused the kitchen. A newly purchased plastic trashcan, with the price tag still on it, was sitting behind the center work island that was basically a slab of scarred pine and square legs. I picked around in the trash with my gloved hand. An empty frozen dinner tray, some kind of spicy food with smoked paprika, according to my nose, sat on top of a moldy half loaf of bread and an apple core. There was only one dinner tray, so it seemed Lionel had been eating alone. He certainly didn't have the elegant gourmet food taste I would have expected.

The rim of a glass peered out over the lip of the sink. I walked over and was pleased that I'd made the journey. A half filled cocktail glass sat next to an empty water glass. The inch or two of liquid left behind in the cocktail glass was pink, just like the one the woman on *Funtasy* was sipping when I saw her sunning on the deck.

Even with a gloved hand, I didn't dare touch what I considered to possibly be significant evidence. The glass of pink liquid could prove that the woman from the boat, Lionel's third female friend, was inside Lionel's house sometime this evening. Connecting a suspect to a crime scene was very important. I nearly skipped with giddiness to the service porch where Briggs had stayed an inordinately long time.

"I've found something," I said, excitedly as I rounded the corner.

Briggs was taking pictures of the door jamb. It had been splintered into wooden shards.

"Oh wow, you found something too," I said as I walked up behind him. "I take it those giant splinters aren't just normal wear and tear."

"Definitely not. Someone pushed this door in." He moved the door aside to point outside. "I'm guessing they used that cinder block to do it."

"Probably a good guess. So it *was* planned. The killer showed up here with the intent to shoot Lionel dead."

"Could be. It's also possible Lionel didn't know the killer or did know them but would never have invited them inside. Apparently, they never thought to try the unlocked front door."

I touched Briggs' arm. "James, is it possible this was a random killing? Maybe someone came here to rob the place. After all, one would expect to find expensive art and treasures inside a house like this, even as rundown as it is."

"And with the Porsche out front," he added. "But what thief goes through the trouble of shooting someone and then leaves the victim's wallet untouched?"

I shrugged. "Maybe he couldn't find the wallet?"

"Maybe, although Gillum said they found it on the sofa in the sitting room. There isn't much furniture or personal belongings in this house. It would have been easy to find."

I sighed. "Yes, that makes sense."

"I noticed you switched to the pronoun *he*," Briggs noted.

I blinked at him. "My goodness, you are pronoun centric this evening. But mostly I've switched to *he* because I'm picturing a possible thief instead of a jilted lover. And I just think that a thief is more likely to be a man because, well men are just more—"

"More dissolute?" he offered.

I tilted my head side to side. "That's a strong word, but I guess it pretty much captures my thought."

"You're probably right there. If it was a random killing, that is. But I'm not convinced it was. The crime scene is just too clean. No struggle, no overturned furniture, what little there is. The only thing that's out of place is this broken door."

"Well then, if we're off the random killer notion, which thank goodness we are because those are much less fun, then I've found something that could be important."

Briggs followed me to the sink. He stared into it, and the anticipated puzzled brow followed. "It's a pink cocktail," he said plainly.

"With lipstick on the edge of the glass," I noted.

Briggs leaned in closer. "Yep, you're right, and I didn't see that color on the victim, so I guess we can assume he had a female visitor at some point in the evening." Briggs glanced at me and squinted. "You're smiling."

"Yes, yes I am."

"You know something."

I nodded. "Why, yes I do. Remember that woman we saw Lionel kissing this evening, the one on the boat?"

"The yacht?" he asked.

"If you insist but I think it sort of misses the mark. Anyhow, I saw that same woman, stretched out on a lounge on the deck in a glamorous movie star sort of pose with big sunglasses and red lipstick." I motioned to the sink. "This color is more coral. The color she wore on the boat was much more of a cherry red."

"So this drink might have been consumed by someone else?" he suggested.

"On the contrary, Detective Briggs. Most women have a plethora of lipstick colors, one to go with certain moods or the colors of their clothes or whether or not they have a suntan." I waved off my explanation. "No, the important thing about my earlier run in with the woman on the boat—" I sighed in irritation. "We really need to find out her name. Anyhow, when I saw her yesterday, she was lounging with her pink cocktail. It was the same bright pink as the liquid in this glass. She was here. That woman on the boat was here in Lionel's house, having a drink."

"Unless it was another woman in coral lipstick drinking a pink cocktail," Briggs suggested.

"You're just being contrary because you were woken from a deep sleep."

"You're probably right. Anyhow, it's definitely evidence that the team missed." He shook his head. "I'll get them in here to collect the glass. Anything else you noticed or smelled?"

"Do you mean aside from decades old grease and dust?" I crinkled my sensitive nose. "Seriously, there are layers of it in here. I could probably tell you what Mrs. Palmer cooked for Thanksgiving in the year 2000 if I gave it a good whiff."

"Like Officer Gillum said, hope Dexter got a good deal on this place. It's a wreck." Briggs reached for his tie and realized he wasn't wearing it. He stared down at his crumpled shirt with the top button uncharacteristically open. "I'm never going to hear the end of this at the Chesterton Precinct."

"What? That you came to work without a tie and a wrinkled shirt?"

A slight smile formed on his lips. "No, that I showed up to a murder scene with my girlfriend and still only partially dressed in what was obviously yesterday's work clothes."

"Oh," I said calmly, then my eyes rounded. "Oh!" My face warmed with a blush. "Guess it looks somewhat unseemly but then like you said, I am your girlfriend." I reached forward and straightened his crooked collar. "I can't decide which moniker I like better, girlfriend or investigative partner."

"Assistant," he said.

"If you say so, but I did just discover a major piece of evidence. Think I'll survey a few of the other rooms and see what the *professionals* missed." I tossed a teasing glance over my shoulder. "Might even find the murder weapon." I added a haughty swing to my hips as I left the kitchen.

Most of the rooms along the hallway that jutted from the main area, namely the kitchen and front room, where Lionel's body was discovered, were empty. There weren't even the obligatory unpacked boxes one would expect to find when someone recently moved into a house. A slightly open door led into what must have been the previously mentioned sitting room. The floor to ceiling dust crusted windows looked out over a weed choked yard, which included a long since dry fish pond and a fountain that was crumbling from decay. A rather unfashionable brown and green sofa sat in the center of the mostly empty room.

It was easy to assume that the evidence team didn't need to spend much time in any room since there was so little furniture and clutter. It made for an easy inspection. It also made for a rather disappointing crime scene. There were no interesting smells, or at least none that I could smell over the victim's powerful cologne. It seemed there was no real evidence of any kind.

The only light in the room was coming from the coroner's bright lamps down the hallway. The room was filled with shadows of the overgrown trees outside the windows. I walked to one of the tall windows and gazed out over the moonlit patch of weeds. It certainly was a fixer upper. If Lionel was as wealthy as Kate had purported, then why on earth did he latch onto a place that needed so much work? Maybe he saw its potential and for a good price, he decided it would be a great investment. Wealthy people never needed to worry about renovation costs. A big budget could have eventually turned the place into a palace. Only, sadly, it seemed the old house wasn't going to get its chance to shine again.

I swung around and my eyes caught a tiny sparkle in the otherwise dark room. It had come from the sofa. I hurried over and knelt down in front of it. My body produced another shadow, this time over the couch, but in the darkness, something glittered. I took my glove out of my coat pocket and pulled it back on. I reached under the sofa and my fingers wrapped around something solid. I dragged it out and turned toward the light streaming down the hallway.

"The necklace," I muttered. "My goodness, I've seen you more often than I've seen any of my own necklaces."

"Who are you talking to?" Briggs' deep voice flowed into the room. He pointed a flashlight at me and quickly lowered it when I had to raise my arm to shield my eyes. "What do you have there?" He came into the room.

I pushed to my feet. "Your *assistant* just found another very significant piece of evidence . . . I think."

He pointed the flashlight at the necklace on my gloved palm. "Where did you find that?"

"Under the sofa. I just happened to see the little diamond glitter in the light coming down the hallway."

Briggs pulled an evidence bag and pen out of his pocket. He began to write down the necessary details on the outside.

"Aren't you going to ask me why I think this is significant?"

"Well, the fact that someone apparently threw or hid a necklace under the couch means it could have been there because of a fight, or Lionel was trying to hide it from someone."

"Yes, there's that," I said, flippantly. "Or it could be that this was the necklace I saw Lionel buy in Lola's shop. The expensive antique necklace he bought for Margaret Sherman, the widow he was dating. I saw her wearing it and bragging about it earlier today when I went into Elsie's bakery."

His eyes lifted. "You're sure about that?"

"Positive. You can ask Lola just to be certain, but it's an unusual, one-of-a-kind necklace." I snapped my fingers, suddenly remembering something. "Margaret Sherwood lives nearby. Possibly even this same street."

"Good work, Lacey. That's all information I wouldn't have had if you weren't always flitting about town."

"Thank you very much. I'm happy to flit whenever it's required."

CHAPTER 14

*N*evermore had woken me from a sound sleep. In my tired stupor I'd accidentally, or quite subconsciously, turned off my alarm rather than hit the snooze button. Thankfully, a hungry cat could serve as an excellent back up alarm. He was quickly dismayed at me for practically throwing his cat food at him as I rushed around like a nutcase trying to get ready. I texted Ryder to let him know I was running very late. Awesome guy that he was, he texted back no hurry. He had everything under control.

Kingston hated it when I was rushing and anxious. He churned himself into his own nervous dance. His talons scraped on the top of the car seat as he moved back and forth along it, letting me know, in no uncertain terms, that I had irritated him. He was also angry that I didn't have time to cook him his usual hardboiled egg breakfast. In fact, the more I thought about it that was probably a greater source of his irritation than me rushing around with my hair on fire.

My tires chirped a little as I pulled up to the curb and parked. I opened the door and Kingston and I flew out, the bird literally and me . . . well, my arms were sort of flapping. We almost always had a morning rush, people buying flowers for coworker's birthdays, teachers, and other daily occasions that required a nice bouquet, and I felt guilty that I'd left Ryder entirely alone for the busy period. It was hard to both wait on customers and arrange the flowers.

Kingston had had enough of me. He shot straight into a tree, letting me know he had no desire to sit in the flower shop with a crazy woman.

I pulled open the door, still in a frenzied state but was immediately calmed by the sight of Ryder leaning casually over the work island, sipping a coffee and chatting with Les. The leaf and ribbon debris on the island assured me it had been a hectic morning, but, as usual, Ryder had handled it all with ease.

"Oh my gosh, what will I ever do without you, Ryder?" I said as I hurried past to put my things in the office. "Morning, Les," I added as I disappeared around the corner.

"Morning, Lacey," he called back. "Brought you a gingerbread latte to try. It looks as if you might need it."

I shoved my purse in the cupboard and a carton of yogurt in the mini office fridge, then raced back out to the comfort of my gingerbread latte. I grabbed it and took a sip. Instantly, all the anxiety of the morning melted away. "Hmm, Les, this is wonderful. Transports me right to a holiday morning, cozy in my pajamas and sitting by the tree. You are a lifesaver." I pointed at Ryder. "And so are you, you terrific, wonderful, amazing assistant."

"You forgot talented, handsome and, uh, a pretty good skateboarder," Ryder said.

"And I'm sure there are at least a dozen other appropriate accolades, but my head is still too foggy to come up with them."

Les pushed the sleeve of his sweater up. "I take it you were out late investigating the murder."

I lowered my coffee cup. "You know about it?" I asked, stunned that the news had traveled so fast.

"Sure. That's the nice thing about owning a coffee shop," Les said. "You get to hear all the latest news as early as five in the morning. Customers from Chesterton were all a twitter about the murder at the Palmer house. Gunshots, death, a mysterious new stranger, intrigue, all the stuff to make a morning over coffee cups that much more enjoyable."

"I suppose all the police activity in such a quiet neighborhood doesn't go unnoticed. I'll clean up from the morning, Ryder. You take a break." I started cleaning the work island.

"Is it true the victim was Kate's new boyfriend, the rich guy with the expensive car?" Ryder asked. He hopped on a stool to take a much deserved rest.

"It's true. Has anyone seen her? I was in such a hurry this morning I didn't even glance at her shop when I drove past."

Ryder looked at Les and they both shook their heads. "She hasn't been in for her usual coffee," Les said. "Which reminds me, I own a coffee shop. Better get back."

"How is the new barista working out?" I asked. Lester was much less picky about his workers than his sister, Elsie, but he occasionally hired people too fast and then regretted it later. This time it was a young man who was just starting city college. He seemed bright and nice.

"He's great so far. No complaints but we'll see. The good ones usually move on quickly." Les walked out and popped back in. "I see a certain detective heading this way." The door shut and he headed back to the coffee shop.

"I wonder if James is feeling as groggy as me. I think he dropped me off home just before five in the morning."

"Jeez, no wonder you overslept. You hardly had any time in bed," Ryder noted. "I've got to take a bunch of potted herbs down to the Corner Market. Tom and Gigi wanted some sage and thyme to place with their Thanksgiving display. I've already put them in my car. Do you need anything while I'm down there?"

I'd heard most of what he said, but things were still processing slowly. "How about a clear head? Preferably one that got a few hours more sleep."

"I'll see what Gigi has in her clear head aisle. Too bad the Uptons don't sell those smelling salts they used to use in the nineteenth century to arouse a woman who had swooned. With your nose, one whiff could probably send you straight to the moon." He laughed at his theory as he headed out the door.

Just as Les had mentioned, the bell rang and a *certain* detective walked inside. He looked far more awake than I felt. He was back to a tie and buttoned shirtsleeves.

"I found myself drifting off over paperwork, so I decided to take a brisk walk down the street to visit my favorite florist." He instinctively walked to Kingston's perch but was just out of it enough to not notice it was bird-less. He stared at the empty perch. "There's no bird." He pointed at Kingston's favorite end, then turned back to me. "There is usually a pushy bird standing right here. Unless I've been imagining it all this time. Which might be the case."

He seemed to catch me standing in somewhat of a daze with a dust broom in my hand and headed across the shop to me. He took the broom from my hand, placed it on the counter and pulled me into an embrace. "I saw Ryder leaving so I'm taking advantage." He kissed me. "That was a thank you for helping last night."

He lowered his arms, and I involuntarily sighed in disappointment. I could have just stood in his warms arms for a few hours and taken a nice nap.

"I came to fill you in on a few details about the case," he said.

"Yippee. What did you find out?"

"First, the obvious. Victim died of a gunshot to the chest. According to ballistics, the killer used a small handgun, a Glock 42, easy to hide in a purse or deep pocket. Unfortunately, there was no sign of the weapon in or around the property. Mr. Dexter, if that's his real name, died between eleven and midnight, which we already knew because that was when the neighbors called the police to report a gunshot."

"Interesting." A tap on the door signaled that my crow had returned from his tantrum. I walked to the door to let him in. "Especially the little side note you added about Lionel Dexter not being his real name," I continued.

Kingston marched in, wings tucked back, like a short, chubby man dressed in black and walking purposefully with his hands behind his back.

"That is one angry bird. What did you do to the poor guy this morning?" Briggs circled around to the treat can, hoping to win some favors with the bird while he was still mad at me.

"I accidentally turned off the alarm. If Never hadn't swatted my cheek with his paw, demanding to be fed, I might very well still be curled up under my quilt dreaming of Elsie's sweet cakes and my boyfriend's even sweeter kisses."

"Glad to know my kisses are swirling around in there between strawberry buttercream and German chocolate. Anyhow, the reason for my side note is that when we looked to notify next of kin for Mr. Dexter, we couldn't find anyone. He seems to have no connection to the outside world, which usually means he was running under a fake name. Which makes this next detail more plausible but equally stunning. The Palmer house is still in a huge probate struggle between family members. It was never sold. Mr. Dexter never purchased the property."

My hand flew to my chest. "He was just squatting there? Guess that explains the lack of furniture."

"It might also explain why the back door was broken," Briggs noted. "And why he left the front door unlocked. He had no keys."

"Of course that all makes sense. Oh my gosh, Kate is going to hate to hear all this. She went on at length about his wealth. What about the Porsche?" I asked.

He nodded. "He had leased it from a dealer under the name Lionel Dexter. Apparently, he had the required fifteen thousand for the down payment on the lease. So they were eager to hand him a contract. But he paid the deposit in cash, according to the dealership. However, he was already late on his first lease payment."

"I suppose that's not too surprising." I picked my hand broom back up and began sweeping leaf and stem litter into a dustpan. "What's next on our investigative list?" I asked with enough enthusiasm to assure him I wanted to be included on all of it.

He couldn't hold back a grin. "I've got a few things to do, but I'm planning to go interview some of the neighbors." He pulled out the evidence bag with the necklace. "I'm heading across to Lola's right now to get a positive identification on this necklace. Because I have to cross all my t's," he said quickly before I could assure him I was right. "But if you can get away after lunch, you can go with me on the interviews."

"And the woman on the boat, with the pink cocktail?" I asked.

He headed to the door. "She's on the list to be talked to. The boat is still in the slip, but there wasn't anyone on board this morning. I'll text you when I'm ready to head to Chesterton. Unless I fall asleep on my desk, which might very well happen."

CHAPTER 15

he wealthy neighborhood where the Palmer house stood was much more beautiful in daylight, especially minus the red blinking lights and the police activity. The only sign that something horrible had happened in the tree-lined neighborhood of stately homes and lush green lawns was the yellow caution tape still draped across the front door of the crime scene. As it was, the neighbors were probably tired of the vacant house, with its weed riddled, mostly dead landscape and deteriorating facade. Now, the house had brought something sinister to their upper crust, seemingly peaceful neighborhood.

A trio of people stood under a sprawling elm two doors down from the Palmer house. They had that drawn, worried look that one could expect from people whose night had been interrupted by a gunshot and murder. They stared at us as we drove past and pulled up to the Palmer house.

"Something tells me if any of the Palmer family ever shows up here at the house, they are going to have rotten eggs and tomatoes thrown at them. This house sure stands out, and not in a good way," I added, unnecessarily.

"I know there have been several heated city council meetings about it, but there's not much anyone can do and the feuding family members live in different states. When they get word that a stranger was living in the house and later wound up dead on their family room floor, they might find a way to settle their differences and finally unload the property. Of course, I'm not so sure people will be clamoring to buy it."

We climbed out of the car. The weather was somewhat dreary, gray and cloudy, not bright and crisp like the past two days. It was appropriate weather for a murder investigation, and the right amount of gloom to match the mood of the neighborhood.

"Guess we could start with the three people standing under the elm. See what they heard and saw that might have been unusual on their street," Briggs said.

I stretched my legs to take longer steps to keep up with his official *detective's* stride. Two women and a man, who all looked to be in their sixties or early seventies, stood beneath the halfway naked branches of the tree.

They eyed us with a touch of suspicion as we headed toward them. "Afternoon." Briggs immediately flashed his badge. "I'm Detective Briggs," he said.

One woman pulled the collar of her coat closed and smiled. "Of course, it's you, little Jimmy Briggs. My husband, Dr. Freemont, was your pediatrician when you were a little boy. I knew you were a detective now, but this neighborhood hasn't ever had anything terrible like this happen so I guess we've never seen you around these parts."

Briggs flicked his gaze my direction, no doubt to see my reaction to him being called little Jimmy Briggs. I was, of course, enjoying watching him squirm.

"How are you, Mrs. Freemont. How is Dr. Freemont?"

Her face softened. "I'm afraid he passed away five years ago. Sometimes doctors are too caught up taking care of patients, and they forget to take care of themselves. But thank you for asking anyhow, Jimmy. I mean, Detective Briggs."

"I'm sorry to hear that, Mrs. Freemont," he said.

"Guess you're here to investigate the murder," the man said. He was wearing a black wool hat, and a big red scarf was draped around his neck. His thick chin rested on the red wool as he peered out from under the brim of the hat. Something about his whole look reminded me of Frosty the Snowman. "Have they found the killer yet? None of us can rest easy until the person is behind bars."

"We're working on it, Mr.—" Briggs paused to let him fill in the blank.

"Hart, Bradley Hart."

Briggs pulled out his notebook. "If you don't mind me asking a few questions, I'm trying to find out if anyone noticed anything different on the street yesterday. Particularly around the Palmer house. Any cars that aren't usually around? Any people that seemed out of place?"

The second woman seemed to have a better grip on the cold weather than her two bundled friends. She was wearing just a thin blouse and a pair of black pants. "We sure did. All three of us noticed a small red car parked in the driveway yesterday evening. Must have been around six because that is when I cook dinner. I can see the driveway from my kitchen window."

"And your name?" Briggs asked.

"Sandra Tuttle. Uh, this won't go in the paper or on some list, will it? We're already concerned enough about a killer running loose. We certainly don't want any trouble." She looked rightfully scared.

"No, Mrs. Tuttle. This is my personal notebook. It helps me if I need to come back and ask you more questions and if we need potential witnesses."

I knew the last part would shock her, and the flicker of fear in her eyes confirmed my prediction. Briggs reacted quickly to assuage her concern.

"This is still all preliminary, so there's no need to worry. However, anything you can tell me will help us catch the killer quickly." He turned back to Mr. Hart. "Anything you can remember about the car?"

"I didn't think enough about it to give the car a good look," said Mr. Hart, "but if my memory serves me right—" he chuckled, "which it doesn't always, believe me. But I think it was a red Honda."

"Kate's car," I blurted without thinking.

Everyone looked at me.

"This is my assistant, Miss Pinkerton," Briggs said.

"Do you know who was driving the red car?" Mr. Hart asked.

"Oh, not necessarily." I quickly backtracked. The last thing I wanted to do was toss Kate out there as a suspect. It was rather unthinkable, but there I was thinking about it. "I just happen to know someone who drives a red Honda."

Briggs snuck a sideways glance at me before writing the information down in his notebook.

"Aren't you that nice, young woman who runs the flower shop in Port Danby?" Mrs. Freemont asked.

I smiled brightly. "Yes, that's me."

She turned to her friend. "I bought the loveliest bouquet of pink carnations from her when Minnie was in the hospital for her gall bladder attack."

Briggs cleared his throat to get them to focus on the case.

"Norris lives right next to the Palmer house, on the other side," Mr. Hart piped up. "He said he saw Margaret Sherwood wandering around the front yard, trying to get a look in the windows." He pointed to the neighboring house on our side. It was a large Tudor style home with thick swaths of ivy growing along its facade. "Margaret lives right there. Haven't seen her yet this morning. She usually has lunch with her sister in Mayfield on Wednesdays."

"You mentioned Norris?" Briggs asked as he wrote down the name.

"Yes, Jack Norris, but he left early this morning," said Mr. Hart. "He's helping his son restore an old house near the coast. He'll be back later. But he said it was very strange. He couldn't understand why Margaret would be snooping on the new neighbor. He pulled on his coat to go outside and make sure she was all right." He glanced at his two friends. They all cast a knowing look around their circle. "We always worry about Margaret. She's never quite been the same since Charles died."

Mrs. Freemont confirmed with a grim nod. "It's true. She nearly lost her entire fortune to an investment scandal. Fortunately, Mr.

Escobar, who lives just down at the corner, got wind of what she was doing and stopped her before she gave everything away to some crooks."

"Did Mr. Norris ever find out why she was wandering around the Palmer house?"

Mr. Hart shook his head. "He said she saw him coming across the yard and hurried back to her own house and shut the door." Again, all three cast a concerned glance around their half circle.

"Did all of you hear the gunshot?" Briggs asked next. The question caused them all to blanch a bit. It must have been very alarming.

"It certainly woke me," Sandra said. "Sent my cat right off the bed. He hid under it for a good hour afterward. Now, mind you, I was deep asleep, so I wasn't totally sure about what I'd heard. But then I noticed Jane's light was on." She motioned toward Mrs. Freemont.

"That's right. We called each other to confirm what we both heard. We live right across the street from the Palmer house." Mrs. Freemont pointed to two stately homes that sat side by side. They looked as if the same architect had designed and built them at the same time. She shook her head. "That house has been a blight on this neighborhood since Thomas Palmer died."

"It's those darn children," Mr. Hart piped up. "Dennis and his sister, Mindy, never got along, and I'm afraid Thomas died suddenly and didn't have his affairs in order. The whole estate was in a mess. We were all pleased to discover that they had finally come to an agreement and sold the place. We were looking forward to seeing the house being restored."

"It's certainly been like an ever present, unsightly weed in this neighborhood," Mrs. Tuttle said. "Now it seems we are back to square one."

Mrs. Freemont's face snapped her direction. "Sandra, we are way behind square one. Now we have this scandalous event taking place. We're a neighborhood plagued with murder. Our home values just dropped significantly."

"Now, I don't know about that," Mr. Hart jumped in.

Briggs cleared his throat politely to remind them he was

conducting an investigation. "There were multiple calls just after midnight to the police station to report the gunshot. Did any of you make a call?"

Slowly, they all nodded. "I suppose we should have coordinated it so only one of us made the call," Mr. Hart said. "But we're just not used to hearing gunshots in this neighborhood."

"Most neighborhoods aren't used to it," Briggs reminded him. "Thankfully," he added.

He flipped closed his notebook. "You have all been very helpful. Thank you for that and we'll keep you posted."

"Hope you find them soon," Mrs. Freemont called as we walked away.

"Just how long had Kate been dating this man?" he asked as we headed back to the car.

"I'm not sure. She came into the shop Monday morning to tell me about him, and the way she was talking, it was already serious. However that doesn't mean much because she's gotten engaged to men she's only known a month." We stopped and I looked at him before climbing into the car. "You can't possibly think Kate is a suspect."

He shrugged. "Haven't ruled anyone out at this point. But I'm definitely going to have a chat with her."

CHAPTER 16

$\mathcal{T}$he afternoon layer of clouds had disintegrated, leaving behind a blue fall sky. So when Ryder asked if I'd take a few more herbs down to the Corner Market, I was happy to oblige. Apparently, the sage had been a big seller for people making their Thanksgiving lists.

Ryder loaded up the little red wagon we used to pull half-off plants out onto the sidewalk with newly potted sage. The scent of sage could occasionally be too musty, almost skunk-like to my sensitive nose, but the fresh, leafy plants Ryder had placed in small red pots reminded me of my mom's holiday cooking. I pulled on my coat, grabbed the wagon handle and headed out on my sage delivery mission.

With the cloud cover gone, the temperature had dropped significantly. My nose and ears were instantly cold. I stopped to lift up the hood on my coat, and as I did, my gaze inadvertently floated in the direction of Kate's shop, Mod Frock. Her sidewalk chalkboard announcing the day's deals and the small rack she rolled out to go with the deals had been put away. The sidewalk in front of her shop was empty.

My wagon rattled and wobbled behind me as I circled it around and headed to Kate's store. There was a sign in the window that said 'closed for the rest of the day' and the shop was dark. It wasn't terribly surprising. I was certain this whole thing had hit her hard. First, she learned Lionel was seeing another woman, then the man ended up dead. It was a lot to absorb. I was sure Briggs would quickly determine that Kate had nothing to do with Lionel's death. She had motive and witnesses did see her car at the murder scene, but it was still too crazy to even consider that Kate had killed Lionel.

I turned the wagon around again, never an easy feat with a wagon filled with potted plants, then headed toward the market. It was cold enough that I walked most of the way with my face down to avoid making my eyes water from the chill. My downward gaze served a purpose in more than one way. I was also able to keep better track of cracks, ruts and other obstacles along the way, thus keeping my wagon from pitching sideways and spilling the breakable clay pots.

I knew, by the scent of onions in the air, that I was passing Franki's Diner. I reached the corner where Harbor Lane made a turn to become Pickford Way. I looked up just long enough to make sure it was safe to cross, then carefully rolled my wagon down the sloped sidewalk and crossed over to the Corner Market. I was still keeping my face out of the bitter cold when I nearly collided with a customer leaving the store. The woman gasped and dropped her paper bag. A few of the oranges rolled free.

"Oh my gosh, I'm so sorry. I was looking down to avoid the cold," I huffed as I ran after two of the oranges. I plucked them up and turned back to the woman. It was my turn to gasp. The woman I'd seen on the boat, the pink cocktail drinker, straightened from picking up her fallen bag. She was wearing large, dark sunglasses and a short leather coat trimmed with fur.

She grabbed the oranges from my hand and stuck them in the bag. She glanced nervously around as if she was worried someone was following her, then she took off on shiny blue high heels without a word.

"Again, I'm very sorry," I called to her, but she never turned back around.

I walked into the market. My head momentarily swirled from the onslaught of aromas, everything from spicy sausage and ham that the owners Tom and Gigi Upton sliced paper thin behind the deli counter to the sweet citrus scent wafting from the mountain of glossy, dimpled oranges sitting in the front bin of the produce aisle. Our freshly potted herbs had been neatly arranged around a rustic wicker basket overflowing with butternut squash, pumpkins and chestnuts still in their smooth, mahogany shells.

"Hello, Lacey, thanks for bringing those." Gigi was wearing a sweater with a colorful turkey. She'd pulled on black shoes that had big silver buckles in perfectly Pilgrim fashion. "People have been buying up the sage like crazy."

I helped her carry the sage over to the window display.

"I was keeping my face down to avoid the cold," I said, "and I sort of collided, actually it was a near miss, with your last customer. She wasn't very willing to accept my profound apology."

Gigi moved a few of the thyme plants around and pushed the new pots into place. "Yes, she's sort of an odd bird. She's been in here twice this week and is rather unfriendly. Not sure if I've ever even gotten a hello out of her. Today, she seemed anxious or worried about something. I know she's staying on one of the boats in the marina."

"Yes, I've seen her on a boat called *Fantasy*." We finished putting the last pots on the shelf.

"Have you seen Kate today?" I asked. "I noticed she closed up shop early."

Gigi tapped her chin. "Hmm, not sure. Hey, Tom," she called toward the back of the store.

Tom appeared with a matching turkey sweater, but instead of shiny buckle shoes, he was wearing a Pilgrim hat. It suited him. He was pushing a rolling cart piled high with butter leaf and romaine lettuce. "Hello, Lacey. Everyone loves your herbs."

"That's wonderful, only I have to give all the credit to Ryder because it was all his idea."

"Tom, have you seen Kate today? Lacey said she closed up her shop early."

Tom thought about it, then shook his head. "Can't say I have."

Gigi turned to me. "I hope she's all right. It's not like her to close up early. Tom and I have been so busy getting the store ready for the holidays, we've been sort of out of the loop. However, I did hear someone say Kate had a new boyfriend."

"That's hardly news," Tom muttered, not really intending for us to hear.

Gigi frowned at him. "Anyhow, I hope she's not sick."

"I'm sure she's fine. I'll see you later. Just give us a ring if you want any more herbs."

"Will do. Bye, Lacey."

CHAPTER 17

J toddled out of the market with the empty wagon bouncing and squeaking behind me. I giggled to myself thinking about how it must look—a grown woman walking along with her empty toy wagon. Only it wasn't empty long. I felt a light tug and turned around to find my crow sitting on the edge of the wagon, going along for a ride.

"King, what have I told you about hitchhiking?" I quipped just as two women were walking past. They smiled weakly at the odd woman scolding the crow. And here I was wondering what people would think about me dragging around an empty toy wagon.

The wind was not nearly as cold and biting going back toward the shop, so I was able to keep my face up and, hopefully, avoid running into angry, flustered people with grocery bags.

Wings flapped behind me. I looked over my shoulder as Kingston lifted into the air and took off toward the beach. I had a spare few minutes and decided to follow him. I was *that* mom, the one who kept a tracking app on her wayward, rowdy kid. There was hardly anyone on the beach this time of year, so the seagulls wouldn't have left behind any potato chip or sandwich crumbs. I was interested to see what'd caught his attention this time.

My little wagon danced cheerily behind me as I headed along the wharf to the steps that led down to the beach, the direction I'd seen my daft crow fly. I decided not to put the wobbly wheeled wagon through the torture of a stout flight of warped wooden stairs. I left it behind and trotted down the steps. It seemed I'd been wrong about the seagulls. A large group of them, frenzied and flapping, were just finishing an impromptu picnic, provided to them, by none other than Heather Houston, the photographer. She stood nearby by with an empty wrapper and looked on, with a small degree of horror, at the melee she'd started with her leftover sandwich. She backed out of the way of the wild wings and circled behind her tripod, where her camera sat ready to go. She took a few quick pictures of the seagull frenzy.

Kingston was perched on the edge of a nearby trash bin waiting for his chance. I knew, too well, that he was well fed, but Ryder and I had concluded this was just one way for him to still act like a bird. Something he occasionally liked to do.

"Did you get a good shot?" I asked, startling Heather.

She pushed a curly strand back into a hair band and smiled, though it wasn't exactly genuine. It looked a little forced. "Not sure if there's such a thing when they're all flapping their wings at each other. I made the mistake of tossing my crust to one lone gull that had been hanging around watching me take pictures of the ocean. Next thing I knew, there was an entire flock of them dropping down from the sky." She noticed Kingston. "It seems even the crows have arrived."

"Crow." I held up one finger. "He's with me and he's sort of a loner."

She looked rightfully confused, but she didn't ask me to clarify. A gust of wind brought a spray of salty seawater. "I suppose I should shut down for the day. I'm pretty much finished with this stretch of the coast. I'll be moving north soon." She walked around to her camera bag sitting on her coat. She lifted it. There were some photos piled underneath the bag. "I printed a few shots of Marty and his lighthouse. Would you like to see them?" she asked.

"Absolutely, I'd love to." I walked toward her.

The gulls had finished their feeding frenzy, but Kinston remained on his trash can. It seemed, once again, I was *that* mom, the one who tagged along to the school party to check up on him and ruin all his fun.

A gust of wind whirred along the sand just as Heather handed me two pictures of Marty and the lighthouse. They blew out of our grasp and I gave chase. Somehow, I managed to snag one picture from midair, and since I didn't want to stomp on the second one, I dove for it, landing solidly on my knees in the sand. I managed to snag the second picture before it took off toward the rocks.

The words high gloss were printed on the back of the photo paper. I turned them over to blow off the sand. Marty's kind gray eyes smiled up at me. He looked positively miniature next to the lighthouse. The print quality was not the best. The blue ocean looked sort of a sickly green, and the shiny black roof on the lighthouse looked more like gunmetal gray.

"I'm glad you caught those," Heather said. "Not that I'll be using those, obviously. I just printed those on my crummy little printer. But I'm sure Shuster Publishing wouldn't be too pleased if some of the photos got out ahead of the book."

"These are great. Marty is beaming with pride." I handed them back to her. "Shuster? That's a pretty big publisher. You'll get big distribution with them. Are they lining up book tours? It seems the people who you meet on your photographic journey would love to see you again at book signings. I know Port Danby citizens would love to see their favorite lighthouse in your book."

She pushed the pictures into her coat pocket. "I'm sure they are planning lots of promotion, but unfortunately, the editor has the last say on which photos make the cut. I didn't have the heart to tell Marty that there's always a chance the Pickford Lighthouse won't make it into the book."

"I'm sure it will." I glanced in the direction of the lighthouse. "After all, it's the best lighthouse on the coast. Of course, that's my biased opinion, but I know everyone here would agree."

"Well, it's been nice talking to you. I need to clean up for the day. I think I've taken about all the photos I can of this beach."

"Yes, nice talking to you. I should get back to work too." I turned around and headed up the steps with my crow keeping an eagle eye on me. I reached the top and looked back. He swept over the sand to look for crumbs. Yep, I was spoiling his fun. I had to stop being *that* mom.

CHAPTER 18

*N*evermore had curled up next to me on the couch for warmth. The chilly fall day had turned into a glacial winter-like night. As the sun had dropped from the sky, a drizzly fog crept on shore, smothering the town with its frosty droplets.

I'd wisely decided to buy some apple cider on my way home, so I could brew up a spicy hot cider for couch sipping. My nose hovered in the warm, clove filled steam long enough that I could taste the spice without even sipping the cider. The scent was strong enough to make my nose tickle.

I picked up my book just as my phone rang. It was my mom. I'd been too busy to call her this week, so I was probably in for a guilt inducing lecture.

"Hey, Mom, sorry I didn't call—"

"Do you remember Kaitlyn Beckman? You used to take dance classes together when you were little."

"Yes, I remember Kaitlyn. I went to two of her slumber parties. She always cried when she lost a game. In fact, she cried a lot, about everything. Why are we discussing Kaitlyn Beckman?"

Mom sighed dramatically. "She's engaged."

"Wow, with that sad sounding sigh, I thought you were going to tell me something terrible happened to her." I knew of course that the sad sigh was because yet another one of my neighborhood friends was getting married before me.

"No, nothing terrible at all. I ran into her mother at the grocery store, and she couldn't wait to relay all the wonderful news. Apparently, he's a lawyer who is joining a big firm, and they just put a down payment on a sprawling ranch house in California."

"That's very nice, Mom, but I'm not entirely sure what I'm supposed to do with that information."

Mom huffed loudly. "Nothing, I just thought it was interesting. Another one of your school chums is getting married."

"We weren't really chums. We were just sort of people who hung out in the same circle. Like I said, lots of crying. How's Dad?" We needed a topic switch.

"He's fine but this cold weather is starting to make his knees hurt. I told him all those years on the golf course had ruined the cartilage in his knees. Are you keeping warm?"

I chuckled. "Nope, I wore my bikini top to work this morning just for the heck of it. And right this minute, I'm standing barefoot on the front porch."

"Such a funny girl," she said wryly. "Now, you're still coming home for Thanksgiving, right?"

I dreaded even thinking about being anywhere near an airport during the holidays, but I'd made the promise back in summer. I believe it was a topic switch back then too because the first half of the call had been about Olivia, my old friend from school, getting married to a podiatrist.

"I'll be there. I'm looking forward to seeing you guys, but James isn't sure he can get all those days off."

A long disappointed grumble followed. "It would be nice if he could make the effort. He hasn't met the family yet."

Yes, all part of my plan, I thought with a grin. "Mom, he's the lead detective for three towns. He plays a pretty important role in the safety and security of this area. He's going to try and get it off, but no promises on that yet. You'll just have to be satisfied with boring old me."

She clucked her tongue. My mom had a plethora of sound effects for phone calls so there could be no misreading her feelings about things. I missed her next Mom-ish comment when the conversation was interrupted by a knock on the door. The unexpected knock, along with my startled reaction, sent Nevermore off the couch and down the hall to my bedroom.

"Mom, I've got to go. Someone is at the door." I got up from the couch.

"At this hour? Don't open the door to any strangers, not at this hour. Not at any hour. Should I tell your dad?"

I couldn't stop the chuckle. "I think he might be a bit too far away to do anything about a stranger showing up at my door. I hopped up on my toes and peeked through the peep hole. "Besides, it's not a stranger. It's my neighbor, Dash."

"Oh, it's Dash." Her voice got a little fluttery. She, like most women who met Dashwood Vanhouten, was instantly smitten, even though she knew the entire scandalous story of Dash betraying his best friend, James, by having an affair with his wife. Still, Mom always sounded a little more frivolous whenever I brought up my remarkably handsome neighbor.

"I'll talk to you later, Mom." I hung up and opened the door.

Dash was holding a piece of mail. "This ended up in my mailbox." He took a deep whiff. "Why, dear neighbor, have you been baking?" he asked with his incredible smile.

"Only if you count stirring some mulling spices into cider, baking. Come on in. There's enough for one more cup and it's still warm."

I headed into the kitchen. Dash pointed toward the tarp hanging over Kingston's cage. "I guess this is how you get the guy to sleep at night. I don't think I've ever been over here this late."

He reached the kitchen. I handed him a cup of cider. He took a second to warm both his hands around the cup.

"That cold snap sure came in fast," he said. "Hmm, delicious. Hits the spot perfectly."

We headed out to the living room. I sat on the couch and picked my cider up, while Dash sat on the chair adjacent to the couch.

"Sorry for coming here so late, and it wasn't really just about the mail." He took another sip and lowered the cup. "Kate stopped by earlier this evening. She was pretty upset."

I scrunched my face. "About the new boyfriend? I'm sure it was a big shock to her."

"Yeah, you know Kate. She meets a man, goes on one or two dates and she's picking out wedding china. I think that's the main reason she can't seem to hold on to the right guy. She's just too pushy. I don't think she was dating this guy for more than a week or two. He only just arrived in town a month ago, or at least that was what he told her. Turns out he was quite the jerk."

I leaned forward to place my cup on the table. "I guess the necklace clued her in to the whole scandalous affair."

Dash looked puzzled. "She didn't mention a necklace, however she did show me a picture of the guy walking along the wharf with another woman. Someone slipped it under the door at Mod Frock. Lionel and the woman were holding hands."

I sat up straight. "Did you see the picture? Has she shown it to the police? It could very well have to do with the killer."

"I don't think she's shown it to the police yet. She had it crumpled up in her purse. I only glanced at it, but the woman was wearing big, round sunglasses. It looked like she had streaks in her dark hair."

"The woman on the boat," I said with a clap, then shook my head. "I've really got to found out what that woman's name is. It's not very investigative of me to keep referring to her as the woman on the boat. It lacks a certain finesse." I sucked in an enthusiastic breath. "Wait, you've probably seen her boat down in the marina. It's called *Funtasy.*"

Dash chuckled at the name. "I would definitely remember that one, only I've been working over in Mayfield helping to restore a 1900 steam yacht my client bought at an auction. It's been murder finding parts for it. Speaking of murder—" He smiled. "Like how I did that? Clever, considering I've been up since four in the morning."

"You get a big gold star for the day," I said. "Now what about murder? You know it's my favorite topic. Did Kate have any suspicions about who might have killed Lionel?" With any luck, I'd get some insider information directly from Kate through one middleman. And all for the price of one cup of cider.

"Actually, she's worried that she might be a suspect. She said she got a voicemail from Detective Briggs asking if she could come to the station tomorrow to answer some questions about Lionel Dexter."

I bit my lip, feeling a moment of Kate's angst. "Is she freaking out?"

"That'd be a good way to put it. I told her she had nothing to worry about, unless she was the killer."

My eyes rounded. "You didn't say the last part, did you?"

"Why yes, yes I did because I'm an imbecile. I thought a little humor would help, but it was definitely not what she needed to hear. She sobbed for a good five minutes."

I tried to visualize Kate sobbing, but I just couldn't get an image. She wasn't exactly the sobbing type. She was tough, almost strident in everything she did, but it seemed she had a soft, vulnerable side too.

"I'm sure James will just ask her what her relationship was with Lionel and when she saw him last." My hands flew to my mouth. "I nearly forgot. Lionel's neighbors, who really aren't his neighbors." I waved my hand. "Another part of the story but anyhow, the neighbors told James there was a red Honda in Lionel's driveway the night he died."

"Kate didn't mention she went to see him. She told me she confronted him about the picture, but stupidly, I didn't put two and two together. That's not going to help her."

"But the car was gone long before midnight, when the gunshot was heard. So unless she drove back later, it still doesn't put her at the crime scene at the time of the murder."

Dash grinned. "Look at you, sounding all official."

I brushed some invisible dust off my shoulder. "Thank you, I've been working on my investigator's vernacular. Except that whole 'woman on the boat' thing. I've got to find out her name," I said more to myself than to Dash.

Dash drained his cup and stood up to carry it to the sink. "I need to get to bed. I can barely see straight, and the alarm is going off at four again."

I got up to walk him to the door. "I can't imagine climbing out of bed while it's still dark and heading out into the pea soup fog on the coast to start my day."

"That's where my gigantic thermos of scorching hot coffee comes into play." He stopped at the door. "Good night and I hope you catch the killer soon."

"Ten-four. Wait, is that right? Doesn't matter. Good night, Dash."

CHAPTER 19

*J*ate a sensible breakfast of oatmeal and fruit, knowing full
well, that my good intentions would probably be obliter-
ated by one of Elsie's Thursday morning chocolate cranberry scones.
They were a hot item at this time of year, so I'd left Elsie with a
standing order to put one aside for me. But to further my good intentions, I followed my healthy breakfast with a brisk bike ride.

An aqua blue sky with puffy white clouds covered the town and
the sun had lent enough warmth that I decided to ride to work.
Kingston had no interest in flying to town. He saw me pull on my
bicycle helmet and dashed back into his cage.

I pedaled down Myrtle Place, glad that I'd remembered to pull on
my gloves. The sun had warmed things up, but riding against the wind
was chilly. My sunglasses kept the wind from burning my eyes, but
my nose was numb. I glided downhill past Grayson Church and its
cemetery. I was just about to pedal past when I noticed the
groundskeeper was cleaning pigeon droppings off the stone angel in
front of the Price family burial vault. It was positioned on a small
grassy knoll above the rest of the graveyard. I'd made several trips to
the cemetery, focused mostly on the Hawksworth family plot, and, in
particular, the small unmarked grave next to the rest of the family. No

one seemed to know who was buried in the unmarked grave, and I hadn't, yet, uncovered the mystery. But after my visit with Marty, I was newly focused on Jane Price and her field of lavender. Did Jane write the lavender filled love letters to Bertram? I badly wanted to find the answer.

Fortunately, I'd made enough visits to the cemetery to get to know Chuck, the groundskeeper. He was a big, silent guy who rarely smiled, but he never seemed to mind answering a few annoying questions.

Chuck was wearing his signature work coveralls, dull gray to match the stones on the church. It seemed this fine morning he had the unenviable task of scraping bird poop off porous stone statues. Being rather an expert on cleaning up after a messy bird, I felt a great deal of sympathy for the man.

He was scraping away with a tiny metal chisel when I walked up. I cleared my throat, deciding I might startle him if I just walked up and said his name. He didn't hear me over the scraping sound.

"Good morning, Chuck," I said brightly.

He looked up at the stone face of the angel he was cleaning, then he looked back over his shoulder. Relief washed over him. "Lacey, it's you. I thought the angel said my name. Thought maybe it was my time."

"Oh gosh, I'm sorry about that. Still, I'm glad it's not your time. I saw you chiseling away on that statue. I always wear something around my nose and mouth, like a bandana, when I'm cleaning up after Kingston. That way the powdery debris doesn't get sucked into your mouth."

He lowered his tool. "That's probably a good suggestion, but after ten years of cleaning these statues, I think I'm immune to whatever gets sucked in." He glanced over at the side of the cemetery road where I'd parked my bicycle. "Did you ride all the way up this hill just to tell me that, or is there something else in that curious head of yours?" Chuck always liked to get right to the point. I decided to do the same, only I wasn't sure if he was going to go along with my request.

"Would it be terribly inconvenient if I took a quick tour around the vault? I'd just like to see how the famous Price family rests in peace, as they say. I'm sure they must be buried in style."

"Not as fancy as you might think. They had plenty of power, those Price men, but they were never all that successful in business," Chuck said.

"That's interesting. Still, I'd love to just take a quick look around." I motioned toward the massive loop of keys on his belt. I flashed him my most enthusiastic smile. It seemed to do the trick.

With some hesitation, he reached down to the loop of keys and unclipped it. "Just a quick look, mind you. I'm almost done here, and I've got a dozen more statues to clean."

I nodded sharply. "I promise. Just a quick look around. Besides, it's probably not all that inviting in there," I added.

"Not unless you like cold, dark and musty smelling places," he quipped as he walked to the arched black door that led into the vault. I expected a few minutes of searching for the correct key, but he produced it with hardly any effort and unlocked the deadbolt. "Just a few minutes," he reminded me. "I'm going to keep working and make sure no one from the church walks this way. Not sure how I'd explain this little field trip."

"You're a peach, Chuck. I'll be right back." I pulled my own keys out and turned on the fairly powerful penlight my dad had insisted I always carry on my key chain. It had come in handy far more times than I expected, which made me feel extra silly considering the fuss I'd put up about hanging the thing on my keys.

An instant shiver went through me as I stepped into the main chamber. It wasn't just from the cold. It was always slightly alarming to see stone sarcophaguses just sitting inside a room like pieces of furniture. Chuck had been right. There were no special adornments or gold plated angels or any of the other fru fru things one might expect in a powerful family's tomb. Harvard Price had a simple block of stone with his name carved in it.

The smell of hundred-year-old dust and decay was already starting to penetrate my sensitive nose cells. I hurried around the chamber and directed my light at each stone. Fielding Price was buried next to his wife, Charlotte Price. His daughter, Henrietta, was buried next to Charlotte. His son, Denton, and the current mayor's father had his own section of the tomb. His wife, Claudia, was entombed next to him, along with a smaller sarcophagus for a daughter named Brenda. From the dates on the headstone, she'd only lived to the age of ten. Mayor Price had suffered the tragedy of losing a sister early in his life. I supposed that would help me respect him a bit more.

I walked back over to Harvard Price. There was no sarcophagus for Jane Price. His own daughter did not make the cut for the family vault. Or maybe she preferred not to be buried with the rest of them. It was entirely possible that she had moved away and married and was now resting in a cemetery next to her husband.

"Lacey? Are you finished?"

"Yes, coming right now." I was just as glad to step out of the cold, dark tomb and back into the sunshine. "Whoa, that place can make you feel really gloomy. Does it ever get to you?" I asked. "Working in a cemetery?"

He shook his head. "Nope. I used to work in a factory where machines were pounding on metal all day. This is the quietest place on earth."

"That makes sense. Well, thank you so much for allowing me to take a tour of the tomb."

"Find anything interesting?" he asked.

"Not sure but hopefully." I waved to him and hurried down to my bike. Once again, I was late for work. But it had been a productive morning nonetheless.

$\mathcal{M}$y gloves proved to be a little thin for the bike ride to town. The brilliant sunshine had turned out to be somewhat deceiving, which was my fault. I knew well enough that sunshine in late fall was quite different than a full day of sun in August. My fingers and nose were so cold from the ride that I determined wrapping my fingers around a cup of hot coffee, all the while resting my numb nose in the warm, fragrant steam, was just what I needed. I parked my bike in front of the shop and circled around to Les's coffee shop.

Much to my surprise, my very handsome boyfriend was sitting at one of Les's pub height tables warming his own hands and nose with a cup of coffee. "I came here looking for you, but your shop wasn't open yet." He glanced at his watch. "You're late."

"I'm well aware of that. I decided to ride my bike to work today and made a little pit stop." I held up my hands, still covered in the inadequate gloves. "My fingers are numb, so I need to wrap them around a hot coffee."

He pushed forward a second cup of coffee. "I bought you one, but it might not be as hot as you hoped."

"Any bit of warmth should help." I picked up the cup and pushed my nose closer, hoping to warm it up. It filled with the rich aroma of Les's special roast coffee, but it seemed the only thing that was going to defrost me this morning was my warm shop. "Thank you for the coffee."

He stood up and we walked toward the flower shop. "Where's the bird?" he asked.

"He decided he wasn't up for a flight to town. He prefers to travel by automobile." My fingers were still too stiff to unlock the door. "I think my bird had a good point this morning." I handed Briggs the key to open it.

"What was the pit stop?" he asked as we entered.

I walked straight to the thermostat and tapped the heat higher. "I stopped by the cemetery," I said as I headed down the hallway to put away the backpack I'd used to carry my things on my bike. I walked back out with my coffee.

"You sure do love that creepy old cemetery," Briggs noted.

"It's not creepy. It's—It's, well, I guess it's a little creepy. But there's so much history there, and this morning I treated myself to a personal tour of the Price family crypt."

He laughed, then saw that I was serious. "You toured their crypt?" he asked.

"I did and it was rather plain and uninspiring, but I found out something interesting. Jane Price was not buried next to her father, Harvard. All the other children, daughters included, are tucked in next to their paternal counterparts, but Jane is nowhere to be seen."

He shrugged. "Could be she married someone far away from Port Danby and is buried with her husband. Don't you think you might be straying off on the wrong path with the Jane Price connection to the Hawksworth murders? I mean a sprig of hundred-year-old lavender is hardly evidence."

"I guess we'll see once I solve this case." I flashed him a cheeky grin.

He chuckled. "I like your attitude. You're right. I guess we'll see."

"Help me pull some flowers out of the cooler. I need to put together some everyday bouquets. Then you can tell me what's going on with the Lionel Dexter case."

"We're trying to find out who owns the *Funtasy*, and we're having a hard time tracking down the woman who was living on the boat. It's especially hard when we don't have a name or any information about her."

I nearly spilled the bucket of carnations I was carrying. "I saw her. I saw the woman." We put the flowers down on the work island. "In fact, I smacked into her and caused her to drop a few oranges. She was quite frosty in our exchange. I kept apologizing but she had no response. She was definitely distracted, almost nervous, as if worried she was being followed." I motioned for him to follow me back to the cooler for more flowers. "Maybe she was worried that the police were looking for her, which I guess they were."

"She was in the Corner Market? I've got a full-time watch on the boat, but she hasn't shown up. I'll have to ask Gigi if there was a credit card used on the transaction. Thanks for that." He placed the tall vase of day lilies on the island. "I've got to head back to the station. I'm waiting for Kate Yardley. I've asked her to come in and answer some questions."

"Yes, she's quite distraught about it. Which reminds me of something else. Now, let her bring it up first because I was told by someone who Kate confided in."

"Dash," he said, dryly.

"Yes but do you want to hear this or not?"

"Yep, go ahead." His demeanor always changed when Dash's name came up.

"Apparently, someone sent Kate a picture of Lionel walking on the wharf, hand in hand with the mystery woman."

"Mystery woman?" His brows bunched.

I sighed. "The woman on the boat. I was trying to use a different title for her rather than the long, pedestrian 'woman on the boat'. I thought mystery woman sounded more intriguing. You really need to find out her name."

"I plan to. Who sent the picture to Kate? Sounds like someone was trying to warn her that she was attaching herself to a player."

"That's what it seems like. But she doesn't know who gave it to her. They slipped it under the shop door."

"I guess someone was hoping to get Lionel into trouble. I'll have to ask her about it."

I opened my mouth to protest, but he put up his hand to stop me. He gave me that tilted head, sincere brown eyed look. "Lacey, this is a murder investigation. I'm not going to tip toe around to spare people's relationships. But," he continued before I could put in my two cents. "I will give her a chance to bring it up first." He took hold of my hand and drew me closer. "What I would like to know now is—how the heck do you always stay two steps ahead of me on these investigations?"

I shrugged. "I'm in the community much more than the detective who is always either chained to his desk with paperwork or sitting at the courthouse to testify against bad people." I grinned. "I've got more bridges."

"I suppose that's true." He leaned forward and kissed me. "Stay out of trouble . . . and crypts," he added as he headed out the door.

CHAPTER 21

*L*ola took a bite of her burger. She chewed and swallowed. "Now that you've bribed me with lunch, exactly what sketchy thing are we up to during this lunch break, and why have you involved your best friend in your clandestine activities?" She went in for another bite.

"Well, on a crazy whim this morning, I decided to ride my bike to work. Then, as lunchtime grew near, I got the sudden urge to go back to the scene of Lionel's murder. It happens to be in Chesterton, which is too far to travel on two wheels during a lunch break. Therefore, I needed my best friend to drive me."

She lifted her soda out of the console and took a long draw on the straw. "So you're using me for my car. Anyone could be your best friend today as long as they had a car."

I wiggled my bottom on the passenger seat and sat up straighter. "If you're going to put it in such general terms, then I suppose so. Only, you're the best friend I knew would be happy to drive me as long as there was a cheeseburger included."

She leaned her head side to side. "Good point." She wrapped up the last few bites of burger. "Can't eat another bite. I had two of Elsie's chocolate scones this morning. Feeling a little glutinous." She wiped off her hands and turned the key. "Direct me where to go. I'm now at your service."

"Great. Just go down this road and turn right at the end of it. We're heading to that neighborhood overlooking the bay, the one with all the mansions. That was where Lionel was living when he was shot." I used air quotes for the word living, which rightly confused my driver.

"Why the air quotes? Was he a vampire or a member of the walking dead?"

"No, I might have used those quotes wrong. He was living, of course, but he never actually purchased the house. It's never been on the market. He must have discovered that it'd been vacant for years and just moved himself in."

A short laugh burst from Lola's mouth. "So, Kate's supposedly rich boyfriend was squatting in a mansion. He drove a nice Porsche though."

"Leased, apparently. It seemed he did have some money but not enough to purchase a big home in Chesterton. There seems to be a great deal of mystery surrounding the victim."

"Pull up right here to this sad looking place in the middle of all these splendid homes."

Lola parked the car and we climbed out. "Boy, this place sure stands out like an ugly brown grape in a bright red cluster. I'll bet the neighbors close their eyes when they're driving past it." She followed me across the dead front lawn to the path leading around to the back of the home. "I guess we're not important enough to be invited in the front door."

"I assume the front door is locked, but with any luck, the back door will still be unlocked. Someone, probably Lionel, himself, broke into the house through the back door. They turned the door jamb into splinters."

"Someone? Maybe it was the cold blooded killer?" She grabbed my arm. "Are you sure this is safe? I thought killers always returned to the scene of their crime."

"Only really stupid ones." The back patio was just a puzzle of chunks of cement with weeds popping out of every crack. We stepped over some particularly tall ones and reached the back door. It was slightly ajar.

"Guess we're in luck," Lola said. "It appears to be open."

"I would have expected the police to shut it so that it at least looked like it was locked." I shrugged at their carelessness and opened the door.

"What are we looking for?" Lola whispered.

"Not too sure," I whispered back.

"Why are we whispering?" Lola asked.

"I don't know," I whispered back. "You started it and I just followed along."

Lola laughed. A noise followed that didn't come from either of us. It had come from the room with the sofa. I turned to Lola and pressed a finger to my lips to let her know we needed to be quiet. Although, I was sure she figured that out.

"What if it's the killer, the really stupid killer?" Lola hissed in a quiet but worried whisper.

I put up my hand for her to stop walking, then I crept as silently as possible on creaky floors toward the sitting room. I reached the doorway and peeked inside. Margaret Sherwood stared back at me, frozen to the spot, and white with fear. Her eyes looked close to popping from her face. "Who are you?" she asked in a wavering voice. It seemed we had scared her as much as she had frightened us.

"I'm Lacey. I occasionally assist the police with investigations." I didn't have the time or the wherewithal to come up with an alternative explanation for me to be sneaking around a murder scene, so I went with the truth.

Margaret looked close to fainting. I led her to the sofa. Lola came down the hallway to see what was going on and who I was having a conversation with.

"Margaret?" Lola asked. "Didn't expect to see you here." Margaret shook her head sadly. I was glad to see the color coming back to her face.

"I came here to look for something, something I lost."

"Was it a necklace?" I asked.

Margaret looked as if someone had slapped her. "Why, yes. How did you know?"

"Lacey was in my shop when Lionel came in to buy it for you," Lola said. "What happened to it?"

Margaret rested back to catch her breath. "It was silly of me. But I was angry with Lionel. I actually thought he liked me." Her cheeks reddened. "What a silly old woman I am. I should have known a man like Lionel would never have fallen for me."

I sat next to Margaret. "Nonsense. Besides, you were way too good for the likes of him. Why were you angry at him?"

She sniffled but neither Lola nor I were equipped with a tissue. "He was seeing another woman," she said. "I went out to my mailbox Tuesday morning and found a picture tucked in between the envelopes. It was a picture of Lionel in an embrace with the woman who owns Mod Frock." She sniffled some more.

"There has to be at least some tissue or toilet paper in this house," Lola said. "I'll be right back."

"Don't touch anything else," I called to her. "This is still a crime scene."

She popped her head back in with an annoyed eyebrow arch. "Really? What am I going to touch? The bloodstain on the floor or the crusty dirt that seems to be on every surface of this house?"

"Just go get the tissue." I waved her along and turned back to Margaret. I was hot on the trail of something. I just wasn't sure what. I had definitely uncovered a pattern. "Margaret, do you have the picture? I'd like to see it."

Her shoulders rounded. She looked droopy and sad. "It was too painful to look at. I tore it up and threw it away."

"Is it still in your trash?" I asked, hopefully.

"No, yesterday was trash morning. The picture is long gone. Now the necklace is gone too. I really loved it. I got angry, tore it off and threw it at Lionel before I stomped out of the house. I regretted it instantly."

"Your necklace is safe," I said. "It's in evidence right now, but I'm sure, eventually, you'll be able to claim it."

"Evidence?" She covered her face. Lola returned just in time with a few squares of paper towel. Margaret blotted her face. "That must be why the police want to talk to me. They think I had something to do with Lionel's death. He broke my heart, but I would never kill him or anyone, for that matter." She pressed the paper towel to her mouth and stifled a sob. "Now I've left evidence at the scene of the crime. What a silly old woman I am, and how quickly I fell for his smile and compliments. Never again. I will be alone until the day I die." She sobbed. "I just hope that day won't be when I'm in jail."

I put my arm around her. "It won't be. You have nothing to worry about. Just tell them everything you know. Tell them about the photo even if you don't have it anymore." I helped her to her feet, and we headed to the back door. I paused and looked at her.

"How did you get in?" I asked, casually, so as not to sound accusatory.

She seemed flustered by my question. "How did I get in?" she repeated back my question. The oldest trick in the book for stalling. I knew because I'd used it myself more times than I wanted to admit.

"I—uh—I wandered around to the back and saw that the door was open. I know I shouldn't have been snooping around in the backyard, but I knew the back door was broken. I had noticed it when Lionel first invited me to have coffee. I shouldn't have just walked inside, but I really wanted to find that necklace."

"Like I said, I'm sure you'll be able to get the necklace back once the police have solved the case and determined the necklace had nothing to do with the murder."

She nervously crumpled the paper towel between her hands. "I hope they find the killer soon. This is all so upsetting. I haven't been sleeping at all."

"You might want to mention that to your doctor," I suggested. Lola and I led her over the crumpled patio and through the back gate. "Would you like us to see you up to your door?" I asked.

"No, I'll be fine. Thank you."

Lola and I watched her walk to the brick pathway leading up to her house.

"She did it," Lola muttered quietly.

I looked over at her. "Why do you say that?"

Lola zipped up her sweatshirt. We headed back to the car. We'd used up our lunch break talking to Margaret, and both of us needed to get back to our shops.

"She had motive. Jealousy. It seems as if Lionel really broke her heart. She knew about the broken back door. Or maybe she even caused it." Lola unlocked her car and we climbed inside.

"I'm beginning to think Lionel broke that door when he decided to live in the house. Besides, sometimes it takes a little more evidence than a good motive to prove that you have the suspect," I said. "But that's all right. I can't expect you to know stuff like we professionals." I added in a haughty chin lift.

"You're good at solving murders, I'll give you that. But if you're a professional, then why doesn't Briggs give you a badge?"

I tapped my chin. "Hmm, good question. I think I'll ask him if they have some sort of honorary badge. You know like an honorary degree they give famous people at big name colleges. I'd kind of like to have one just to flash around."

Lola laughed. "I was just kidding, of course. But if you bring it up with James, then please don't tell him that I put the notion in your kooky head."

CHAPTER 22

*R*yder had left early and I was closing up the shop on my own. It was especially quiet because Kingston was still at home. He normally kept me company with his chattering and the click clack of his talons as he followed me around on my closing routine. It had been a somewhat slow day, leaving me with only a few clean up chores. I thought about the case as I finished sweeping the floor.

Margaret and Kate both had motives, although, hardly strong ones. Lionel had not been in town long, so it wasn't as if either woman had dedicated years to the man only to discover his propensity for infidelity. While it was true that Kate tended to grow instantly attached to men, she also grew quite instantly unattached. With the exception of Dash, I'd never known her to pine for any of her ex-boyfriends. She usually moved enthusiastically on to the next guy with barely a flinch. But it was entirely possible that she felt strongly about Lionel. I didn't know her well enough, and we'd never been close friends.

I was deep in my thoughts, absently sweeping the floor, when sirens startled me out of my musings. I rested the broom against the wall and walked to the window. It seemed the activity was happening down at the beach. I popped my head outside. Several emergency vehicles were parked along Pickford Way. It seemed something had happened at the marina.

I raced around grabbing my coat and my keys. When I stepped out of the shop, I searched frantically for my car, only to remember that I had ridden my bike to work. Me and my brilliant ideas.

I hurried back inside, grabbed my bike from the hallway outside the office and rolled it out to the sidewalk. I climbed on and pedaled as fast I could toward the beach. My hands and face were frozen by the time I reached the wharf. Briggs' car was parked near the ambulance. I parked my bicycle and hurried along the wharf. Two paramedics were chatting casually as they pushed their gurney, filled only with their equipment bag, back toward Pickford Way. Either it had been a false alarm or they were not needed because it was too late.

I weaved through the curious onlookers standing in bunches at the entrance to the marina. I searched around for Briggs and spotted him climbing off the boat in the second to last slip. He was talking on the phone. Officer Chinmoor was standing in the middle of the dock keeping curious people from getting any closer to the police activity.

He waved me on. I stopped for just a second. "Officer Chinmoor, what's going on?"

"Murder victim on one of the boats," he said. "Gunshot."

I continued toward the scene and knew even before I reached the vessel that it was *Funtasy*.

Briggs hung up just as I reached him on the dock. "Looks like we have a second victim from the same killer."

I glanced toward the deck and caught only a glimpse of a high heel sticking out of the stairwell that led below deck. "Was it the woman we saw Lionel kissing? I recognize those high heels."

"Yes, we searched around and found a purse with identification." He pulled out a Washington driver's license with the woman's picture.

"Glenda Jarvis," I read. "Well, I was hoping to find out her name, but I certainly didn't want it to happen this way. So, you think it might be the same killer? I mean, I hope so. I'd hate to have to search for two murderers."

"Nate and his team are on their way. We'll need a lab report on the bullet, but the wound looks the same and she was shot at close range in the chest." Briggs motioned me to head over the gangplank to climb on board. He followed close behind. "From the position of her body, it seems the person might have been hiding below, waiting for the victim to head down the steps. She was shot and then fell forward."

We reached the narrow stairwell that led below deck. Glenda was face down sprawled on the steps. A stream of blood ran down the steps, pooling in front of the landing in a dark red puddle.

"The boat is registered to a Marco Plesser. He lived in Oregon, according to the registration," Briggs said.

I looked at Briggs. "Who on earth is Marco Plesser? This whole thing just keeps stretching farther and wider. Is it possible this person, Marco, discovered that Glenda was seeing Lionel, and they absconded with his nice boat? Then he tracked them down and killed them?"

"At this point, anything is possible."

The cold, wet mist over the marina was starting to seep into my bones. I curled my arms around myself for warmth.

"You should head home, Lacey. I know you rode your bike today. It's going to be dark soon. Or I could have one of the officers drive you home."

I shook my head. "No, you're all busy. I won't stay long." I stared down at poor Glenda, lifeless yet stiff, like a discarded mannequin. "Just a few days ago she was sitting out on deck sipping her pink cocktail and now she's dead. Did you get a chance to interview her?"

Briggs pulled out his notebook. "That was how I found her. I came here intending to ask her some questions about Lionel's murder. She was already dead. I think she's been dead for a good twelve hours, which would put her time of death sometime between two and five in the morning." Briggs turned to me. "Lacey, two victims means this person has no qualms about killing people—"

"I know what you're going to say and I'll be careful. I promise." I tapped my nose. "So, should I take Samantha for a spin?" My nose had its very own moniker, and I was quite fond of it.

Briggs smiled. "Wouldn't be a thorough investigation without that. But be careful. There's not a lot of room on the narrow steps."

He handed me some latex gloves, and I pulled them onto my cold fingers. "Someone needs to invent fleece lined latex gloves for cold weather."

CHAPTER 23

There were only a few inches on the right side of the body where I could stand without disturbing Glenda Jarvis, the victim. Briggs had set up the police light, which was like ten thousand light bulbs going off at once in a tiny, dark passage. The glare was almost too much, but it kept me from slipping on blood.

Glenda's head was tilted against the second to last step, mostly facing down. Her eyes were slightly open, making it feel as if she was watching me as I crouched down to sniff her clothes. She was wearing a short, champagne pink faux fur coat and a pair of tight black pants. An outfit like that would have indicated that she'd gone out to a party or dancing the night before but then it seemed she was always dressed for a social event. Glamour seemed to be her everyday look. It was interesting considering that Kate had been dressing down for her new boyfriend, leaving behind her usual flashy mod style for a more staid, collegiate look. I wondered if Lionel was the type of man who played women by telling them how they should dress, even if he had no particular preferences. Sometimes it was just a control thing.

"Lacey, Nate and his team are here," Briggs called down the stairwell. I could only see his outline in the harsh light flowing down the passage.

"Just a minute." The cramped quarters made it hard to get my nose too close, but I quickly picked up the scent of Lionel's expensive cologne. It lingered on her coat but had probably been there for more than a few days since it was faint. That made sense considering Lionel had been dead for several days. It also didn't tell us much because we already knew there was something going on between Lionel and Glenda.

Nate's deep voice poured down past the blinding light. "I hate it when they're on narrow steps," he said. Seemed like a reasonable complaint. It was nearly impossible for me to do a simple nasal inspection. It would be much harder to do a coroner's initial exam. The last thing Nate needed was another person crowding the stairwell. I pushed to standing and climbed back up to the deck.

In the few minutes I'd spent below deck, the sun had dropped greatly. It was definitely time for me to head home. I didn't want to ride back in the dark.

"Why don't I get someone to drive you home," Briggs suggested.

"I've got just enough light to get home safely. But I won't say no to you walking me back to my bicycle. Unless you're needed here."

"I can break away from the scene now that Nate is on board."

He gave me a hand off the boat and onto the dock. He rested his hand on my back, a protective, slightly possessive gesture that I always loved.

"Are you sure you don't want a ride back? It's getting colder by the minute."

"I'll be fine and the chill is nothing a long, hot shower won't erase. Tell me more about today's investigation into Lionel's death, then I'll tell you what happened during my own investigation. Did you talk to Kate?"

We walked through the crowd, which was mostly dispersing because of the cold and the dark. "Kate came into the station looking very distraught. Hilda had to make her a cup of tea to calm her nerves. She said she'd been dating Lionel for about three weeks, and they were quite serious." He flashed an eye roll, but it was pretty much warranted. Three weeks was hardly long enough to become serious, unless you were Kate Yardley. "She'd discovered that Lionel had given Margaret Sherwood a necklace. Apparently, your buddy, Lola, had something to do with that."

"Yes but it was entirely innocent on Lola's part. She had no idea Lionel was seeing multiple women."

We headed along the wharf. The shops and food stands were closing up for the night. I was relieved to see my bicycle was still right where I'd placed it on Pickford Way.

"The necklace didn't matter too much." We stopped at the bike. "Kate turned over the photo. I'm having it tested for prints," Briggs said. "It was definitely Lionel and our newest victim, Glenda."

"I suppose we can take Ms. Jarvis off the person of interest list," I said.

"Looks that way."

"What did Kate say when you asked about her car being spotted at Lionel's house?"

"She was confused and flustered." Briggs took off his fedora and smoothed his hair back before returning it to his head. "She confessed that she drove to his house early in the evening and confronted him about the necklace and the photo. It seems Lionel tried to smooth it over, make excuses. He told her Margaret had been a kind neighbor, and he felt sorry for her being a widow so he bought her a gift. He told her that the woman in the picture was a friend of the family. Kate told him he was a liar and that she never wanted to see him again. She stormed out and that was the last she saw of him."

I could occasionally read his thoughts in his face, but under the failing daylight and the brim of his hat he just looked weary. It had been a long day, and now he would be working late collecting evidence and waiting for the coroner to finish up.

"Do you have any reason not to believe Kate?" I asked.

He shook his head. "Not really. I talked to Margaret Sherwood an hour later. Lionel might have been claiming that he was just buying her a necklace because she'd been neighborly, but as far as Margaret was concerned, they were in a relationship. He took her to dinner several times and whispered in her ear more than once. That part she said with a blush on her cheeks."

"Poor Margaret," I said. "Did she bring up the photo?"

His face popped up. "She didn't mention anything about a photo." His brow perked up. "How do you know about a photo?"

I smiled sweetly. "I might have gone back to the crime scene."

He sighed in surrender. "Lacey—"

I put my hand against his chest. "Before you start the lecture, I just popped in there at lunch. And Lola was with me."

"Yes, that makes me feel much better because the two of you together are such solid, safety conscious decision makers."

"Thank you," I said politely.

"Maybe you missed the sarcasm in my tone," he suggested.

"Nope, I just decided to ignore it and take the whole thing as a compliment. Now, are you interested in my story? Daylight is disappearing fast."

"Yes, go ahead. And make it fast so you can get home. I want a text the second you get in the door."

I smiled. Admittedly, I'd been a little miffed about his sarcastic comment, but it was hard to stay mad at him. "We used the back door to get in the house. It was ajar and I was going to mention it to you because I thought it was rather sloppy of the evidence team but it turned out Margaret was inside the house."

I couldn't see his ears under his hat, but I was sure they perked up. "Really?"

"Yes, she was looking for the necklace. Turns out she yanked it off in a bit of drama, then regretted leaving it behind. I told her it was in evidence, which upset her, naturally, because then she was sure you were considering her a suspect."

"Which we are," he said.

I shot him a surprised look.

"No alibi, she was wandering around his house, apparently snooping in windows and she had motive. Although, admittedly it's a stretch. She seems like a sweet lady. But what about this photo? She didn't mention it."

"It was a picture of Lionel and Kate. Someone left it anonymously in her mailbox. The same person who was trying to warn Kate that Lionel was a cad."

Briggs motioned for me to climb on my bike. "I'll have to ask her for the photo and find out why she failed to mention it."

I threw my leg over. "I think she thought she'd be in trouble. She tore up the photo and the shreds were already picked up with the garbage."

"That won't be much help then."

"You should have your team search for photos at this crime scene. Maybe Glenda received one too."

"Good thinking, Sherlock." He leaned over and kissed me on the nose. "That little button is frozen solid. Hurry home and let me know the second you get in the door."

"I will." I blew him a kiss and took off toward Harbor Lane.

CHAPTER 24

*R*yder was running late due to a flat tire, so I was alone in the shop. Naturally, it was a busy morning. Two separate pairs of customers were browsing my centerpiece portfolios. One pair needed something elegant for a winter social, and the other needed flowers for a sixtieth wedding anniversary. Both pairs were still deep in discussion and debate, so I took a moment to pull our sidewalk chalkboard outside. It was a reminder for people to order their Thanksgiving table centerpieces early. I positioned the chalkboard so that people driving along Harbor Lane could read it.

My gaze inadvertently swept toward the beach. I just happened to catch Heather, the photographer, hurrying across the street to Franki's Diner. Her camera was around her neck, and she clutched her camera bag in her hand. Both objects were somewhat cumbersome, but she managed to get across quickly.

I walked back inside. My customers were still perusing the portfolios. I considered that a good sign. I offered a plethora of beautiful choices, so many that it was hard to choose.

I headed over to the potting station to plant some tiny lavender into pots. I was elbow deep in potting soil when the door opened. "Be right with you," I called.

There was no answer, but I felt a warm presence behind me. I spun around. "James, I wasn't expecting you this morning." I reached for a towel and wiped my hands. "Any news on the latest murder?" I asked as quietly as possible.

Briggs looked around at the customers browsing my bouquet notebooks and motioned for me to follow him outside so we could talk more freely about murder and gunshots.

"It seems we're looking for one killer. The same gun was used to kill Glenda Jarvis. Still no sign of the weapon. Here's more craziness to make this a harder case. Just like with Lionel Dexter, we can't seem to find any family or previous existence of Glenda Jarvis. They both appear to have just popped spontaneously onto earth."

"What about Marco Plesser, the owner of the boat? It seems like he might be key in all of this," I suggested.

"Yes but he's a dead key."

"What? You mean there's a third victim?"

Briggs glanced around as two women strolled past. He nodded and smiled hello, then returned to our conversation. "Marco Plesser died in 2007."

"A stolen identity?" I asked.

The woman who seemed to be taking the lead on the sixtieth anniversary popped her head out the door. "Sorry to interrupt, but we've made a decision."

"Wonderful. I'll be right there." I turned back to Briggs. He had a nice amount of dog hair on the front of his coat. I brushed it off. "Someone got a *Bear* hug this morning before he left the house."

"And a slobbery kiss to go with it. I'm just glad my neighbor has offered to have Bear over during the day to hang out with his dog. I was starting to feel guilty about leaving him home alone so much. Now he can't wait to head over to the neighbor's house."

"I'll bet he loves it. I've got to head inside. Before I do, I'm going to tell you my new theory, in light of this new information."

He smiled. "Looking forward to hearing it."

"Lionel Dexter was one of those terrible men who preyed on vulnerable women, pretending to be in love with them so he could take them for everything they had. Just not sure how Glenda or, whatever her name was, fit into his scheme."

Briggs glanced around and leaned forward for a quick kiss. "Good theory. I think we're both on the same page. If that's the case, he probably had a lot of enemies. I'll let you go sell flowers. See you later. Maybe dinner tonight if I can break free."

"Sounds good. Have a nice day, Detective Briggs."

"Same to you, Miss Pinkerton."

CHAPTER 25

I pulled the long stem rose from the vase and trimmed off the end at an angle to help it take in more water. I stuck it back into the vase and plucked out the next one. After the morning flurry of activity, things had calmed down.

"I think I'm going to just go for it and get a new car." Ryder had been lamenting the old, junky-ness of his car all morning. Since he was saving up for his eventual horticulturist adventure around the world, he was very tight with his budget, but it seemed he couldn't take his old car one more day.

"There are so many of those car shopping sites now, I'm sure you can get a reasonable deal." I grinned over the yellow rose in my hand. "Or why don't you just splurge and get something really fancy and fast. Lola would love it. Of course, that means you'd deplete your savings account and have to start all over again. Which means you wouldn't be leaving me anytime soon, and yes, I'm being selfish but I don't mind. I consider it a worthy cause to reveal the dark side of my personality."

He chuckled. "At least you don't hide behind any fake facade. I'm sure I can find a good deal, something that won't drain my account. I'll start looking when I take my lunch break."

"Good idea." I finished the last rose and was just about to carry them back to the cooler when the door opened and Marty Tate walked inside. He was bundled up in a thick corduroy coat that had worn leather trim on the collar and cuffs.

I circled around the work island to greet him. "Marty, how wonderful to see you." I gave him a gentle hug. "How are you doing?"

"Fine, thanks. The photographer is done taking pictures so the rest of my week has been rather slow. It was such a nice day, I decided to take a stroll along Harbor Lane to visit my favorite florist."

"How nice of you. I have a bottle of water in the refrigerator, nice and cold, would you like it?"

"No, thank you." He unbuttoned his coat but didn't remove it. "Hello, Ryder."

"Hey, Marty, how's it going?" Ryder put down the vase he was filling and walked over for a handshake. "Good to see you, man. You look great."

Marty chuckled. "For a mummy. Truth is, this cold weather slows me down more and more each year."

"Nonsense," I said. "You just walked down here and strolled enthusiastically into the store. There isn't anything slow about that."

"Kind of you to say, but I feel like I'm moving in slow motion on these cold days." He reached into his coat. "I've found a few things I thought you might be interested in, Lacey." He pulled out a small book with a faded green cover. The embossed title had lost its black color, but I could still make it out. *A Handbook of Herbal Remedies.*

Marty handed me the book. "Open the cover. There's an inscription."

I carefully opened the book. A quickly scrawled note had been written on the yellowed title page.

Dear Elizabeth,

I think you'll find this book very helpful. The chapter on cough remedies is particularly good when the winter cold causes a dry throat. I hope you'll put it to good use.

Your friend, Jane Price.

My face popped up. "It's a note from Jane Price," I stated unnecessarily. "It's wonderful."

A half dozen lines creased the side of Marty's mouth when he smiled. It was truly a marvelous smile. "I thought you might appreciate it. I was putting the box of photos away, and I remembered that my mother kept a few personal items wrapped up in a knitted shawl in the closet. This was one of the items she treasured enough to keep tucked away." A boyish grin crossed his face. "She also kept a necklace I made for her from shells I'd collected on the beach. I was eight years old when I handed it to her. I'd wrapped it up in a piece of brown paper and twine. I remember being so excited to give it to her. God bless her, she wore that horrible looking thing to every special occasion. At least until I was twelve and old enough to tell her she didn't have to wear it, which I think I did because I was so embarrassed by the darn thing at that age. She'd wear it and tell everyone I made it for her. That was all right when I was eight but definitely not at twelve."

I could have listened to Marty's charming little anecdotes all day.

"Now, I've got something else to show you." Marty's smile was plastered across his face. He fumbled around in the inside pocket of his coat for a second, even resorting to biting his lip in concentration as he tried to retrieve whatever it was he was looking for. His gray eyes twinkled as he apparently found it. He pulled out another old photo. "When I found the book, I opened it and this fell out. It's an albumen print like the other one, and it's still in good shape because it was protected by the book pages."

It was indeed. The picture was crisp and clear, considering the age and the method of photography. I'd only seen her several times, in an old newspaper photo and the picture at Marty's house. It was Jane Price. She was what people back then would have referred to as a handsome woman. She had nice symmetrical features with large, wide set eyes and fair skin. She was wearing one of the day's fashionable day dresses with slightly puffed sleeves that stopped at the elbow and a skirt that was fitted at the waist to drop slimly over the hips. Only something about her physique wasn't quite right. Jane Price was in no way overweight. Her face was small and slim and her arms looked petite, yet her waist looked too big for the rest of her, even beneath the fitted bodice and skirt. I brought the picture closer to get a better look. She was turned just slightly at an angle with her hand resting on an unopened parasol.

Marty was rightly waiting for some kind of response. "It's Jane Price," I said still studying the photo. I looked up at him. "Maybe it's the angle or the dress but it almost looks as if she is pregnant."

Marty snapped his fingers. "I was thinking the same thing."

"Wow, this is huge, Marty. Maybe that's why Jane was sent away. She was still using the name Jane Price, so I think it's safe to assume she wasn't married. Women carrying illegitimate babies were hidden from public eye or, at the very least, sent off to live away so the family name wouldn't be ruined."

Marty chuckled. "You're pretty good at theorizing this stuff." He noticed Kingston for the first time and walked over to visit with him. He stroked King's head. "You mentioned the letters in Bertram's trunk. Maybe that inscription in the book will match the letters," he suggested.

My feet nearly left the floor. "Marty, you're brilliant. See, you're pretty good at theorizing this stuff too."

He laughed. "Maybe we should become partners, solving all the world's great mysteries."

"Or, at least this hundred-year-old Port Danby mystery. This is great. You've given me some excellent evidence, Marty. I don't know how to repay you."

"Sure you do." He smiled.

"Elsie's lemon poppy pound cake?" I asked.

He nodded emphatically. "Best payment there is."

"Actually, how about lunch at Franki's, my treat?"

"I wouldn't say no to a lunch at Franki's," Marty said.

I patted his arm. "Great, I'll just grab my coat, and we can walk down there together."

CHAPTER 26

$\mathcal{F}$ranki lit up as we walked into the diner. As much as I would have liked to think her enthusiastic reaction was for me, it was all for my lunch partner, Marty. He was quite the celebrity in town. After Franki's hug and a hand flourish showing us the way to what she referred to as his favorite table, nearly every customer in the diner had to greet or shout hello to him. And he took it all in stride with his sparkling gray gaze and kind smile. We sat down at the table, and Franki dashed off to get Marty his usual cup of coffee. She completely forgot the other person sitting at the table until she returned with his coffee, which happened to be in a special blue mug with the name Marty in dark blue lettering.

"Oh, Lacey, sorry, I didn't ask what you'd like to drink." She looked somewhat embarrassed, but it passed quickly when she turned her attention back to Marty. "I've just taken a hot cornbread out of the oven. Should I bring you a chunk with some whipped butter?" she asked him. (Again, nothing for the woman sitting across from him.)

Marty, being the wonderful person he was, smiled graciously across the table. "What do you say, Lacey? Should we have some cornbread and butter to start?"

"Yes, that sounds perfect, Marty." I shot a slightly annoyed look at Franki. "Hot tea, please."

"Sure thing. I'll be right back with that cornbread." I had never witnessed Franki being anything but herself, a plainspoken, sharp business woman who somehow managed to keep her life moving smoothly along, even as a single mother of four teens, but she winked rather flirtatiously at Marty before bustling away to get his fresh cornbread.

I sat up straighter so I didn't have to talk too loudly over the chorus of conversations surrounding us. "Why do I feel as if I just walked into this diner with George Clooney?"

Marty chuckled. "I think people get excited when they see me because that means I'm not dead yet. It's more like a woo hoo, there's Marty, still kicking around and breathing."

I pressed a hand against my mouth to stifle my laugh. His droll humor was nothing short of charming. (Maybe I had walked in with Clooney.)

In what I would label as the quickest service ever, Franki swept right back with a small basket brimming with cubes of steaming corn-bread and a bowl of her special whipped butter. My hot tea was nowhere to be seen.

Franki snapped her fingers. "That's right, Lacey, you wanted hot tea. Be right back with that." I wasn't counting on it.

"I hear there was a murder at the marina." Marty offered the basket to me first before taking one for himself. He pushed the butter bowl my direction too.

"Yes, a woman who was visiting on a boat called *Funtasy*. She wasn't the first victim though. There was a murder in Chesterton earlier in the week, a man who was also new to town."

Marty clucked his tongue. "I sure miss the days when people weren't always getting killed."

I slathered butter on the bread and pushed the bowl his way. "What time period was that, exactly?" I asked wryly. "As I recall, this entire town's tourist appeal is based on an infamous murder."

He nodded once. "So true. Then I suppose it's better to say, I wish there was a time when people weren't getting killed."

We both chuckled and took a moment to enjoy the cornbread. Franki returned. Surprisingly, she remembered the tea. "Guess you two should decide on lunch before you fill up on all that cornbread," she noted.

"I'll have some of your vegetable soup," I said.

"Hmm, that sounds good. Make it two," Marty said. "And a tuna melt."

Franki smiled. "Be right back with that."

"Have you seen the photographer?" I asked. "Or has she left town already?

"I'm not sure. I know she was finished with the lighthouse pictures. Funny thing, this morning I was taking a walk to the market, and I spotted her heading across to the wharf with her camera and her big black camera bag. I waved and called hello, but she was so preoccupied by something she didn't even look to see who was calling her name."

"Maybe she didn't hear you." I sipped some hot tea.

Marty nodded. "Could be. My voice is always a little hoarse in the morning. Comes from all the years of living in a damp filled house. That coastal fog knows how to get through every crack and crevice. Maybe she was just too wrapped up in her book deal with Ballard Publishing."

"I think you mean Shuster Publishing." I had little self control when it came to Franki's cornbread. Who was I kidding? I had little self control at all when it came to yummy treats. I reached for another square and was slightly disappointed that the cornbread hadn't stayed magically warm in the basket. I glanced up from buttering my bread. Marty was scratching his chin in thought.

"No, I'm certain she said Ballard Publishing. Don't know how I would have come up with that name otherwise. I don't know much about the publishing world."

I sat back, genuinely perplexed. "How weird. She told me Shuster. I wonder if she just got mixed up."

"Maybe," Marty said. "Although, it seems like a sort of strange thing to mix up."

Franki returned with the soup. "Here you go, Marty, topped with a sprinkle of cheese and toasted croutons just the way you like it." She placed my unadorned soup unceremoniously in front of me and dashed away.

I smiled behind my hand. "If I didn't know any better, Marty, I'd say Franki has a crush on you."

He shrugged. "Not surprised. It's the Tate curse. Women just can't get enough of us."

We both had a good laugh as we sat forward to eat our soup.

CHAPTER 27

Ryder had headed out to test drive a car he was hoping to buy. Earlier in the afternoon, a frazzled mother had walked in with two school aged kids. She needed centerpieces for a club meeting she was hosting. The kids, who were bouncing around, happy to no longer be sitting in their school desks, were making it hard for her to concentrate on her task. Then a tap on the front door signaled the return of a certain shop mascot. Kingston had taken off when Ryder left, but he returned quickly, apparently not finding any activity to his liking outside the shop. His timing was perfect. The kids spent the rest of the time dropping treats into his tray and watching him eat them. It was rare but my bird actually reached a saturation point on the treats. But he had kept the kids entertained enough for their harried mom to choose orange and yellow carnations for her centerpieces. The group left and Kingston settled down for a long nap, leaving me alone to think about the murder cases. Normally, by now, I would have at least a semi-solid list of suspects, but there was only Kate and Margaret. I was having a hard time trying to picture either of them as a cold blooded murderer. Kate had opened up her shop this morning and was back in business, complete with a new sidewalk sale sign and a display of cool mod frocks to go with it. It seemed her interview at the station must have eased her mind about being a possible suspect. I'd contemplated walking down the street to chat with her for all of a minute. There had never been a great bond between us, and I was sure she'd consider me to be prying. Which, technically, would be right. It was one thing to sort of push my way into talking to a suspect when I didn't know the person well, but it was another thing when that person was a neighboring shopkeeper who I had to see almost every day.

I headed into the office to order the carnations. I sat at the computer. Rather than open my purchase order file, I went straight to Google. I was interested to find out whether Heather Houston had signed a deal with Ballard or Shuster. Not that it mattered much, but it did seem strange that she'd told Marty and me different publisher names.

I typed in Heather Houston, certain that whichever publisher it was, there would have been a press release or some sort of news article about the forthcoming book. There was a lawyer named Heather Houston, and a singer in an indie pop band went by the same name. I decided to take a shortcut and go straight to Ballard Publishing. They had a list of books due out in the next year. I read through the list but saw nothing about a lighthouse photo book and, more importantly, nothing from Heather Houston.

I moved on to the Shuster Publishing site. Their site was a little harder to navigate, but a few clicks and some serious scrolling earned me no reward. There was no mention of an upcoming book from photographer Heather Houston. I tried a few more keywords like lighthouse, coffee table book, coastal scenery but nothing took me to a mention of Heather's upcoming book. I had never asked her when the book was due out. It was possible that the estimated publishing date was two years away. After all, a book of photographs would take a great deal of preparation and work to produce. On top of that, Heather still seemed to be moving up the coast for more pictures. I had to give her the benefit of the doubt that her book was still in the early stages of creation, and there was no mention online because it was too far in the future.

The only question I couldn't reason away was why she would tell me it was a Shuster publication when she told Marty it was Ballard. Something wasn't quite right with any of her story. Since she was quite possibly long gone from Port Danby, I would probably never find out just what the heck was going on.

I was just about to stop my procrastination and start my purchase order when the bell rang on the front door. The clanging was followed by the distinct aroma of cinnamon, which meant that Elsie had arrived with a baked good. The carnations could wait.

CHAPTER 28

*E*lsie strode forward with a plate in her hand. "Nothing too special, just an apple cinnamon muffin. I wanted the display tray to be symmetrical and this one was extra."

"Well, hooray for symmetry." I took the plate. "I think it might have to be dinner. I went to lunch with Marty Tate, and the two of us finished off a basket of cornbread that could have fed an entire fire station filled with hungry firemen."

Elsie hopped on the stool. "Did you just say you had lunch with Marty Tate? Lighthouse Marty?" Her forehead bunched with disbelief.

"Marty is helping me with the Hawksworth investigation. It turns out his mother, Elizabeth, was friends with Jane Price."

Elsie blinked at me. "And that's good because . . ."

"That's right. I guess I've never filled you in on the thread I'm following in the murder case. Jane Price was Mayor Price's daughter from a first marriage."

Elsie nearly slipped off the stool. "Harlan Price was married before and had a daughter?"

I put my hands on my hips. "Elsie, have you been sipping that coffee liqueur again? How could Jane Price be both Harlan's daughter and friends with Elizabeth Tate? Different centuries, remember?"

She waved it off. "Right. Sorry. Guess I'm tired. I need to go for a good long run."

I laughed. "Not many people I know follow the words 'I'm tired' with 'I need to go for a long run'."

"They should. There would be a lot less tired, cranky people in the world. Speaking of murders, what is happening? I heard there was a second victim down at the marina. I'll bet that handsome detective of yours is busy."

"He must be. I haven't heard from him all day. I'm going to drop by the station after I close up to see if he needs me to bring him dinner. Have you talked to Kate at all?"

"She never came into the bakery today, and I rarely have occasion to go into her shop. Her little sidewalk sale seemed to be doing well." Elsie reached down and tied her shoe. "I met the photographer today," she muttered as she was leaned over.

"Did you?" I asked, suddenly intrigued. "I thought she had left town already."

"She came in around lunchtime and bought a cheese filled croissant. She was carrying her camera bag, so I asked her if she was through taking pictures here in Port Danby. She said she was finished with the lighthouse but decided to stick around for one more shot of the sunset on the beach. She mentioned something about fog ruining the last sunset. She plans to move to the next coastal town in the morning." With that, she jumped down from the stool. "Speaking of sunset, I need to go on my run before it gets too dark. Les and I exchanged sibling promises to each other. He is going to eat vegetables and grain three nights a week, no meat, no cheese, no beer, and I promised not to go running after dark."

I walked her to the door. "That's nice. It's good that you two are looking after each other."

"Yep, with Hank all the way in Australia for the next two months and Britney gone to Europe, it's nice to know my brother is keeping an eye on me. Or at least I let him think that, even though it's really the other way around."

I opened the door for her. "Whatever direction it's coming from, it's nice." She was just about to leave when a question popped into my head. Not really sure the purpose for it, but my intuition just nudged it out. "By the way, when Heather, the photographer, came into the bakery, you said she was carrying her camera bag. Was she wearing her camera around her neck?"

Elsie rolled her eyes up in thought. "Yes, I think it was around her neck."

"Interesting," I said. "Well, thanks for the cinnamon muffin. Have a good run. In fact, run a few miles for me, would ya?"

She chuckled on her way out. "If I could do that, I would. I could make a big fortune running for people."

I was still laughing as I closed the shop door.

CHAPTER 29

I locked up and left Kingston napping on his perch. I decided a quick trip to the police station was in order before I headed home. I hadn't heard from Briggs all day, and it wasn't like him not to at least send a text to say hello. I could only assume he was swamped with work, what with two murders and all the other police business he was required to perform. He was just lucky he had me hot on the trail too, I thought with a mental pat on the back. Of course, hot on the trail wasn't exactly accurate, more like lukewarm, and there wasn't really a trail but more like a few scattered stepping stones.

Briggs' car wasn't in front of the station, which signaled he wasn't in the office. I continued inside though, hoping I could do a little snooping in the evidence room. I'd been sort of wound up in my other investigation, the Hawksworth murders, and it had kept me from really digging deeper into the recent murders. I was prepared to go full steam ahead to get these cases solved before I continued on the Hawksworth mystery.

Hilda had been busy stringing up some of her cheesy fall decorations, garlands of fake leaves that, unlike some of the more impressive garlands I'd seen at the craft store, looked truly unnatural. I could have colored leaves on a piece of paper, cut them out, strung them up and they would have looked more real. But it made me smile anyhow. Hilda was always trying her best to make the very plain and stark station office look more inviting.

"Lacey," Hilda chirruped as she glanced over the chin height counter. "If you're here to see Detective Briggs, he was called to the courthouse this afternoon. Boy, was he mad too. Poor guy has so much stuff on his plate. They pull him in far too many directions, if you ask me."

"I agree, Hilda. I suppose Officer Chinmoor is out on patrol?" I asked.

"Yes, although he just radioed that he was taking a dinner break. Oh, would you like to try a piece of my coffee cake? I made it this morning and brought it in. I sent a big slice with James this morning." She picked the plate up off her desk and placed it on the counter. "It's cinnamon streusel," she announced proudly. Hilda loved to bake things. Unfortunately, she was the opposite end of the spectrum from Elsie when it came to baking talent. I couldn't count how many dry, flavorless cookies and crunchy, bitter brownies I'd had to choke down with a smile, all while profusely complimenting her. Briggs thought it might be less dangerous to our health if we just confessed to her that her baked goods weren't all that tasty, but I immediately stopped that idea. So we were forced to continually taste and *enjoy* Hilda's confections. But today, I had a good excuse at the ready.

"I'm sure it's delicious." I took a deep whiff. There was definitely cinnamon, but I wasn't going to be fooled by its mouthwatering aroma. "I can't possibly. Elsie brought me a cinnamon muffin just a few minutes ago, one of her jumbo muffins. It had cinnamon topping just like this cake. I think I've reached my baked good quota for the day. Thank you though. You can tell James that he can have my piece."

Hilda's mouth turned down in disappointment. "Well, all right, if you're sure you've had enough. I know Elsie's muffins are probably way better than my coffee cake."

"I'm sure that's not true." I tried my hardest to sound sincere.

Hilda smiled and picked up the plate. "I guess I'll just give your piece to James. He probably finished the first chunk hours ago, so he'll be ready for more."

I pulled my lips in to fight a giggle. What a stinker I was. "Hilda, I hate to bother you, but do you think you could let me into the evidence room?"

She looked less than enthusiastic. "Oh, I don't know, Lacey, with neither of the boys here, I'm not sure it's a good idea."

"I'm sure James won't mind," I said. "He knows I'm working on the murder cases. He's so busy, I'm sure he'll be extra pleased if I can find something helpful. I only need to see one piece of evidence. I'll take a quick look, then we can lock the room up and that will be the end of it." I gave her my best pleading look over the tall counter.

Her cheeks puffed with a grin. "I guess it couldn't hurt. Besides, I sometimes think you're better at solving these murders than the professionals. I know most of that is due to that powerful nose of yours." She buzzed me through the gate and picked up her keys. "Is it an article of clothing?" she asked.

"I beg your pardon?" I'd gone into sleuth mode, and I was plotting out my next step.

Our footsteps echoed down the narrow, empty hallway to the evidence room.

"The evidence you're going to sniff? Is it clothing?"

"Oh, that. No, actually, I just want to look at something. No sniffing today."

Hilda looked wide eyed at me. "Well, all right. I suppose that can't hurt either." She pushed the key in and fiddled with the lock a few seconds before pushing open the door.

"I'm looking for a photograph from the Lionel Dexter murder investigation," I said.

Hilda and I perused the shelves. The evidence bag with the picture was sitting next to a box containing Lionel's shoes.

"Wait," Hilda said as I reached for the bag. I worried she had changed her mind about letting me see the evidence. She spun around and hurried to the metal table used to examine evidence. She plucked two latex gloves from the box and carried them back to me. "Can't forget these."

"You're right. Thanks." I pulled the gloves on, picked up the bag and carried it to the table. It was a small enough piece of evidence that the table wasn't really necessary, but it seemed Hilda wanted to make sure we did everything by the book. Briggs had allowed me into the evidence room many times. I was sure he'd have no qualms about letting me see the photo, but I didn't want Hilda to worry. I hadn't expected her to stick around but she lingered nonetheless, so I was very slow and methodical about my approach, assuring her I'd done it all before. In truth, the entire process could have taken me just seconds, and we'd already be heading out the door.

I unsealed the bag and pulled out the picture. It had been crumpled at some point, but someone had taken the time to smooth it out so the image was clear. Lionel and Glenda were walking along the wharf, holding hands and seemingly enjoying their stroll. Glenda was wearing her oversized sunglasses, and Lionel was wearing a gray suit, entirely overdressed for a stroll at the beach. That seemed to be his usual style. It seemed he'd decided dapper was the best look for tricking women into loving him. Not that I had proof yet that he was a philanderer, but evidence was sure pointing in that direction.

There were several bright lights above the table that acted like spotlights. I moved the photo under one for a better look. "The photo quality," I muttered.

Hilda leaned over to look at it. "Looks like someone needs a new printer. The blue ocean looks sort of green."

I peered up at her. "And blacks look gray. I know who printed this photo, or at least I'm nearly positive." I was so giddy I surprised Hilda with an impromptu hug.

She pressed her hand to her chest and laughed lightly. "Wow, did we just solve the murder? James will be thrilled."

"Well, we didn't solve the murder yet, but we did solve the mystery of who was delivering incriminating photos of Lionel Dexter to the women he was dating. It's an important step," I assured her.

I realized I had to tamp down my enthusiasm a bit. The photo was only evidence that Heather was the anonymous tipster. There was still nothing connecting Heather to the murder or to Lionel and Glenda except that she happened to take a picture of them walking on the wharf. But why?

I needed to hurry. Heather told Elsie she needed another sunset shot, and the sun was already low in the sky. I pushed the photo back into the bag, sealed it up and placed it right back in the exact same location.

I pulled off the gloves and tossed them in the trash. "Thank you so much for letting me do this, Hilda. I'll let James know I pleaded and begged and wouldn't let you take no for an answer."

We headed out of the room. "I'm sure that's not necessary, especially if this whole escapade helped move the case forward."

We reached the front office, and I gave her another brief hug before heading out the door. I needed to get to the beach and find out what Heather Houston was up to.

CHAPTER 30

$\mathcal{I}$ shoved my hands in my coat pockets to keep them warm and strode purposefully toward the wharf. I wasn't exactly sure what I would say or do when I met up with Heather, but I was sure something would come to me. I was, of course, doing exactly what Briggs always warned me not to do. I was approaching a possible suspect on my own. But it was hard to even consider Heather a suspect. There was seemingly no connection between Lionel, Glenda and Heather. There was no motive. Unless Lionel was seeing Heather too, but I'd seen her around town several times and never noticed her with Lionel. And frankly, how on earth could a man, no matter how big a cad, see that many women in such a small space of time. There just weren't that many hours in a day.

I reached the steps to the beach and gazed around at the sand. No sign of a photographer or her equipment. The sun was still a good half hour away from producing one of its glorious sunsets over the Pacific, but I was certain Heather would need time to set up to make sure she got the shot just right.

The late afternoon wind that usually whipped up as the temperature dropped had slowed to a mild, salty breeze. Thin wispy clouds cluttered the horizon, but no sign of a fog bank. It was the perfect scenario for a beautiful glowing pink and orange sunset.

I didn't want to be caught watching and waiting for her to show up, so I headed down the stairs to take a walk on the beach. I pulled my hood up and tucked my hands in my pockets as I trudged through the thicker, drier sand to the more solidly packed wet sand. Seagulls were still dropping down on the white crests rolling toward shore, hoping to find their last snack before nightfall.

I headed toward the outcropping of rocks below the lighthouse. There was a precariously narrow path that led down from the rear of Marty's house to a tiny stretch of sand and the rocks. When Briggs and I were feeling a little like our teenage selves, we coaxed ourselves into climbing the rocks. They held plenty of critter filled tide pools. It was always fun to watch the sea life going through their daily routines in their shallow, watery world on the rocks.

I was about fifty yards from the outcropping of rocks when a figure emerged on top of them. It was Heather. She was carrying her camera bag but no tripod. It seemed she'd actually put her camera inside the bag for a change, which made some sense because it wasn't that easy to traverse the rocks.

She spotted me and looked confused at first and a little miffed, unless I was imagining the latter. I reached the rocks just as she was climbing down. She gripped her unwieldy black camera bag in her hand as she made the descent.

"Hello," I said cheerily. "We meet again."

Her brows pinched together as she concentrated on her footing. She reached the last rock and stepped off into the sand. "Yes, if I didn't know any better, I'd almost think you were following me." Her tone was not nearly as cheery as mine. In fact, bitter would have been a better word.

I laughed airily as if she had said it in a jovial tone. "Coincidence, I think. I'm out taking a stroll." I squinted out to the horizon. "It's going to be a beautiful sunset."

"Yes, that's why I'm here."

"Guess we should both be careful," I said, again with lightness as if we were just having a nice chat. Occasionally, my friendly attitude helped break the ice, but it didn't seem to be working this time. "There have been two murders in the vicinity," I continued.

Heather took the statement as if I'd just said there were two gulls on the beach. She continued walking so I joined her. "Yes, I've heard. Guess that's a good signal for me to be moving on. I don't like to hang around places where people get shot."

My face snapped her direction. "How did you know they were shot?" I hoped to catch her off guard and fluster her with my question, but she was quite the calm, cool cookie.

"I read it in the paper."

Darn, she was one of the five people in the world who still read a local newspaper.

"Of course, that makes sense." I was hitting a lot of brick walls and awkward silence. I took a deep breath and decided just to go for it. She was already put off by my presence, so I figured I could just add a little salt to the wound.

Heather stopped suddenly. Apparently, she'd found the right spot for her photo. She placed her camera bag on the sand.

"No tripod today?" I asked.

She pulled a bandana from her back pocket and tied up her hair. "Not today," she said curtly.

"Well, then, I guess I'll let you get to work." I pretended to walk away. "Except I did want to ask you one thing."

Her forehead jutted forward in a scowl.

"Real quick question. A friend of mine received a photo the other day. It was left anonymously under her shop door. It showed my friend's new boyfriend walking on the wharf, holding hands with another woman." Her glower deepened so I spoke faster. "She showed it to me. I happened to notice that the ink quality matched the photos of the lighthouse you showed me. Blues faded to green and blacks to gray. You'd mentioned it was your terrible printer."

I expected more anger, her face to grow red and her nostrils to flare. Instead, she lost color in her face. Her defensive posture softened. "You're talking about the owner of Mod Frock?"

"Yes."

Heather nodded. "We women have to stick together, you know?" Suddenly, we were a 'we' and her tone had lightened. "I saw the man in question more than once in my short time here in Port Danby. Each time he was with a different woman. Someone close to me was hurt very badly by a man just like that, so I decided to let the women know."

Her explanation seemed plausible, honorable, even. Had I hit another dead end? A few minutes earlier I practically skipped out of the police station thrilled that I had a solved the mystery of the photographs. I was certain they were connected to the murders, but it was entirely possible they were just a friendly warning to the women that they were being played.

"My friend was upset by the photo, but I'm sure she was grateful for the warning. The woman in the photograph looked very glamorous, as if she had money. I'd never seen her before in Port Danby. Did you send her a photo too? One with another woman?" Briggs' team had searched for a photograph on the boat, one like Kate and Margaret had received, but there was no sign of it. It was possible Glenda had torn it up and disposed of it too.

Even though we had been part of a group, 'we women' just seconds earlier, I felt the cold shoulder happening again. My question had made her clamp her mouth shut into a tight line. "Never got a chance," she said curtly. "I think I did my part. Besides, as you noticed, my printer was running low on ink. Now, if you don't mind, I need to get this sunset shot lined up."

I was being given the brush off, but sometimes I found persistence paid off.

"Yes, for your book deal with Ballard Publishing," I said pointedly.

"That's right." She opened her camera bag and pulled out her camera.

It seemed her book deal was a lie. Either that or she truly didn't know the name of her publisher. Only that seemed impossible. I lingered. (I was an expert at annoying people.) "I see you are finally putting the camera in the bag."

Her face popped up. "That's the usual place for it," she said rather snippily for someone who rarely used the case for her camera.

"I suppose since you read the newspaper, you've discovered that the man who was seeing multiple women was the first murder victim."

She rounded her eyes in surprise but I wasn't buying it.

"How would I know that? I didn't know his name, and they didn't have a picture of the victim in the paper." Darn her for her quick, plausible responses.

"That makes sense. Then I'll let you get to work."

"I'd appreciate that," she said coldly.

I meandered back toward the stairs. I stomped my feet to get rid of the wet sand as I climbed the steps. I glanced back one more time to the beach. Heather was looking at me. She turned away quickly and lifted her camera in front of her face.

I reached the wharf and pulled out my phone. Briggs' phone went straight to voicemail.

"Hey, call me when you have time. You poor man. There needs to be two of you. Oh! I love that idea. Two of you to love. That notion makes my head spin. Call me. I've got all kinds of theories brewing, and I think you might want to hear them. Love you. Bye." I pushed the phone back into my pocket and picked up my pace. I needed to get back to the shop to pick up my things and my bird. Then I had some research to do.

CHAPTER 31

he weather by the coast was so changeable. One minute, a glorious, multicolored sunset painted the horizon and the next, a surly wind carried an angry thunderstorm in from wherever thunderstorms were born. Kingston and I made it home from the shop just as things, namely the sky above, started to get ugly.

By the time we got inside, Nevermore's tail was standing straight up, letting me know static electricity was in the air and his least favorite of nature's music, roaring thunder, was rolling in. (Naturally, his favorite music was the sound of twittering birds because they provided a great deal of entertainment for easily bored cats.)

I'd heated a bowl of lentil and vegetable soup and filled the top with a mountain of salty cracker crumbs. It was the perfect meal for watching the storm roll in. There was still a chill in my bones from my walk on the beach, but the hot soup was doing the trick. The whole adventure had been worth it. My intuition flares were on fire. There was something not quite right about the photographer. With any luck, Mr. Google, an amateur investigator's best friend, would shed some light on the mysterious Heather Houston.

"Heather Houston," I muttered the name before pushing the spoon into my mouth. It was a nice name, almost too nice. Was it possible that Heather Houston was an alias too? It seemed we had a group of strangers show up in town, and all of them were using fake names. I had no proof about Heather's name, but I intended to uncover it. The main snag in all of this was motive. What possible reason could Heather have had to murder Lionel and Glenda? Was Heather seeing him too? There was no evidence to prove that either.

The phone rang as I finished my last bit of soup. "Finally," I said with glee. I answered it. "Where have you been, Detective Briggs? If I didn't know any better, I'd say you were avoiding me."

"Hardly." He sounded weary. "If anything, the only bright spots in my long work day were when my mind was filled with daydreams about you."

I was all alone, but I could feel a blush from my head to my toes. "You were daydreaming about me?" I asked softly.

"I was and I'm sorry there are not two of me. Although, I'm fairly certain if there were, you'd be sick and tired of me by now."

"That is not possible." There was enough background noise that it was clear he wasn't sitting in his car or office. "Where are you? I hear glasses clinking, music and laughter."

"I'm in a restaurant. We just sent a very dangerous drug dealer to prison, and the arresting officers decided to go out for a celebratory dinner. I stepped away from the table to call you but ended up in the noisy bar area."

"Congratulations, James. You're awesome but seriously they need to find you a partner or something because—" I paused dramatically. "Oh wait, you technically have one, and while you're out eating prime rib, your partner is solving murders."

The music grew louder. "Just a second, Lacey. I'm going to move to the front of the restaurant. I'd go outside but it's raining. How about over there?"

"So far just thunder and lightning in the distance but it's coming. Nevermore's tail and my nose tell me so."

Even his deep chuckle sounded weary. "I'm interested to learn what you have on the murder cases. It's probably more than the team I have working on it."

"It's not a sure thing, but let's just say, I'm more than a touch giddy. Are you coming over tonight?" Hearing his voice made me miss him.

"Yes, I need to go home first and take Bear on a walk before it rains harder."

"Sounds good. Why don't you bring him here? We'll lock Nevermore in the bedroom." Nevermore and Bear were still not great friends, but as Bear matured, he grew less wild. And Nevermore was slowly learning not to freak out and run for the nearest tree.

"I'm sure he'd like that, but he's been playing at his buddy's house all day so he might be pooped. I've got to go. I think my food's arrived. I'll see you soon."

"Looking forward. Bye."

A streak of lightning lit up the room causing Kingston, who normally slept like a rock, to pull his beak from his wing. He looked grumpy about the whole thing. I walked over and picked up the cover for his cage. He was still squinting like an angry kid who'd been woken from a nap. "I think there's going to be a lot more lightning, so let's give you artificial night a little earlier than usual. Goodnight, King." He turned his head back to his wing and crouched down as I tossed the canvas cover over his cage.

The thunder was getting louder and coming a little faster, which meant the storm was almost over us. I grabbed my laptop and sat on the couch with my wool throw over my shoulders. I opened the computer and started typing. I decided to head back to the name Heather Houston. I added in keywords like photographer and coastal scenery and several other combinations and finally got lucky. Heather Houston, a Midwest based photographer, had a blog where she posted her photos. Her last post was dated yesterday, and it was a lovely picture of the lighthouse. It seemed she had a few hundred followers. I was sure a publisher would be looking for someone with more of a following but then I didn't know that much about the publishing world.

I skimmed a few of her posts. There was no mention of a book deal. I didn't know much about the publishing world, but I was a hundred percent certain that if she had gotten a deal she would have posted about it. My guess was that there was no book deal. It was entirely possible that she was working to get one, and telling people it was already in the works made it easier for her to get access to the sites. I scrolled through some of her older posts. She'd started the blog about five years earlier. I didn't expect to find anything of note but then something caught my eye. There was a screenshot of a short article from a photographic journal. I leaned closer to get a better look. The entire article was about a fresh, young photographer named Heather Bailey. She was showing big promise in nature photography. It was quite the glowing review. I sat back with a satisfied grin. There was no doubt in my mind that Heather Bailey was also Heather Houston.

I put my laptop on the coffee table and hopped up to grab a notepad and pen. I started writing down all the various names that had come up during this investigation. Starting, of course, with the purported names of the two victims, Lionel Dexter and Glenda Jarvis. There were the two possible but very unlikely suspects, Margaret Sherwood and Kate Yardley. I wrote down Heather Houston and Heather Bailey. I picked up the laptop and started typing in as many combinations of the names as I could but ended up with a lot of meaningless results.

"Poo." I rested back and tapped the pen against my chin. Another jolt of lighting startled me, and I managed to poke my chin with the pen. "Ouch." I rubbed my skin and thought about all the details of the murders, the old, dilapidated house, the luxury boat, the marina. The boat pushed another name into my head. I grabbed the notebook and wrote down Marco Plesser. The boat *Funtasy*, the site of Glenda's murder, was owned by a man named Marco Plesser, who, according to Briggs, was no longer alive. I tried a few combinations, and my last try, Plesser and Bailey typed together, proved fruitful.

I clicked on what appeared to be a three-year-old newspaper report about a woman named Greta Bailey who had tragically committed suicide after a man pretended to fall in love with her. The rotten scammer then proceeded to drain her bank accounts and max out her credit cards. He even talked her into taking all the money out of her retirement account. After the poor woman siphoned off every penny she had to the man who promised to marry her, the bum left town with a full bank account and a brand new car. The man's name was Michael Plesser. He was caught and received only a short six month sentence for wire fraud because the victim, Greta Bailey, had willingly handed over her money.

I laughed dryly. "Which gave him plenty of money for a top notch lawyer," I muttered to Nevermore, who didn't seem terribly interested.

I skimmed the rest of the article. Greta, destitute and heartbroken, hung herself in her kitchen. Her body was discovered by her daughter.

"Darn it." I sat back against the cushion. There was no mention of the daughter's name. Bailey was a fairly common surname. Plesser, however, was not and even though the first names didn't match, I was sure our first murder victim was none other than Michael Plesser or Marco Plesser or maybe neither was his real name. Maybe Marco Plesser was his dad's name and he assumed his dad's identity to buy the boat. It was possible he had dozens of identities. It made sense in his *line* of business, swindling women to hand over their hearts and their bank accounts.

A bolt of lightning caused a moment of power outage. For that quick second, my inexplicable, almost irrational fear of the dark sent my heartbeat into overdrive. I leaned forward to place the laptop on the table, but the follow-up clap of thunder startled me so badly I dropped the laptop the last few inches to the tabletop.

I took a few deep breaths to slow my pulse and was just starting to feel calmer when another bolt of lightning lit up my small house. I raced to the kitchen for my flashlights and candles. Knowing how badly I panicked in the dark, Briggs had brought me several industrial powered flashlights to use in case of emergency. According to my racing heart, this was an emergency.

CHAPTER 32

I sat on the couch with my throw wrapped around me and my flashlights at my side. I hadn't taken the time to light candles because the power was still on, and it seemed like over preparedness even for a nervous ninny like me. Nevermore had decided the storm was just a bit too much excitement for the evening, and he headed into the bedroom for the night. I closed the door so he wouldn't have to deal with Bear too. A thunderstorm and an eighty pound silly dog would definitely be too much chaos for one evening.

The power hadn't slipped on and off since I'd raced to the kitchen for my emergency lighting supply, which helped me return to a calm, only mildly terrified woman. I was certain Briggs would show up soon, then all would be fine, and if the lights went out, well, that might even be fun. (Who was I kidding? Of course it would be fun.)

I picked up the book I'd been reading and opened it to the bookmark. A clap of thunder shook the house, but I was getting used to the noise. Until a different noise startled me right back to a nervous panic. The back door, which led into a service porch and then the kitchen, rattled as if someone was shaking it.

"James, where are you?" I said it out loud, hoping somehow my plea might carry to his ears.

I determined quickly, in order to keep from freaking out, that it had been the wind shaking the door. I pushed the book aside and picked up the heavy, long handled flashlight before tiptoeing to the front window. I used the crook of my finger to slightly part my curtains. I badly wanted to see Briggs' car pulling into the driveway but badly wanting it didn't help.

The back door rattled again. I froze. There had been no gust of wind to go with it. I gripped the flashlight tighter and immediately wondered how much damage it could do to an intruder's skull. A lot, I presumed.

I pulled out my phone and was about to dial Briggs when I heard the door shake again, more violently this time. In my fright, the phone slipped from my fingers. I had no time to call anyhow. Someone was at my back door, and they were trying to get inside.

I turned on the kitchen and the service porch lights, then I aimed the beam of the flashlight right at the sheer curtains on the back door. A shadow flashed by and disappeared. I hurried to the front room. My pulse pounded in my ears, and my throat was so dry I couldn't even swallow to relieve it.

A sound outside alerted me to the terrorizing fact that my intruder had moved to the front of the house. The front door rattled. I lunged for the light switch and threw on the extremely bright porch light Briggs had installed for me. It took all my courage to walk to the peep hole and gaze out but the porch was empty.

I searched frantically around for my phone. When it slipped from my fingers, it managed to slide under the couch. I knelt down, making the pounding pulse in my head even louder. I reached blindly underneath the couch, panicking more with each second. The doors had stopped rattling, but that didn't mean I was safe. The lights might have scared the intruder back around to the dark side of the house.

My fingers finally curled around the edge of the phone. I pulled it out and picked it up. Right then, a knock landed solidly on the door. I chirped a short, dry scream, and the darn phone popped back out of my hand as if it had little rocket boosters.

"Lacey?" Briggs' deep voice pushed a sob of relief from my throat.

He'd used his key to open the door. Beads of water were dripping off his raincoat as he stepped inside with a look of worry. "Lacey? Are you all right? I thought I heard you—" I plowed into him, not giving him time to finish. His coat was cold and wet, but I wrapped my arms around him, holding onto him as tightly as I could.

"I'm all wet," he said quietly as he wrapped his arms around me.

I was trembling enough that he instantly felt it. His hand caressed the back of my head as I pressed my face against him. "What on earth is going on?" he asked.

Now that I was in the safety of his strong arms, it took me only a minute to recover. Once my pulse had slowed and I could no longer feel my heart drumming against my ribs, I peeled myself reluctantly away from his embrace.

Briggs pushed my chin up to look at me. His brown eyes were brimmed with concern. "You look pale. What's happened?"

My body had recovered from the fright, but my throat was still parched. I swallowed hard and took a deep breath. "Someone was rattling my back door." My words sent him straight to the back door. He moved fast enough that a spray of raindrops flew off his coat. I followed closely at his heels, no longer wanting to be so much as an inch away from him and also to keep explaining my ordeal.

"At first I thought it was the wind but then the person kept shaking the door, trying to get inside." He reached the back door, motioned for me to get back and unlocked and opened the door. He disappeared out into the wet darkness for a minute. For that short stretch of time, I held my breath, then released it, loudly, when he walked back inside.

He lifted a metal tire iron. "I assume this is not yours."

"No. That must have been what they were using to try and pry the door open." My throat felt dry again. I turned to the cupboard for a glass.

Briggs locked the back door. "Good thing you only have a small window near the top of the door. It would have been easy for them to break a larger window and just reach inside to open it."

"I scared them off by shining the flashlight out the window. I saw their shadow disappear, and that's when the front door was rattling. I was trying to call you but the phone slipped from my fingers and then —" I pressed my fingers to my lips to keep the first sob from slipping out because I knew once it burst free, the tears would flow. The combination of the lightning storm and the intruder had shaken me to my core.

Briggs pulled off his wet coat, tossed it on the counter and, this time, provided me with a warm, dry hug. It was just what I needed. After a blissful few minutes in his arms, I pulled myself together enough to talk.

Briggs filled my glass with water and led me to the couch. I took several gulps and put the glass down on the coffee table. "I'm sorry I'm being such a cream puff about all this." I hated to show too much vulnerability in front of him because I feared he'd keep me from investigating murders. And I absolutely didn't want that. "It's just there was the thunder and lightning and then the lights blinked on and off. That started my panic mode, then the door rattled." I took another steadying breath. He reached for my hand. It was amazing how much comfort a warm hand hold could give. "Like I said, I thought it was the wind but then it happened again and there was no gust of wind to explain it. I was armed with the big flashlight. I figured I could clobber someone pretty good with it."

The stiff concern on his face finally melted a little. "I'm sure you could. But did you get a look at the person? It'll help if I have a description when I call it in."

"I only saw a shadow. It wasn't very big. I don't think you need to call it in, James. I'm fine. They didn't get inside. You came so quickly after they rattled the front door. Did you see anyone? Any car that was unusual? Maybe someone running down Myrtle Place?"

He grinned slightly. "I like how you spun this around. Now you're the detective questioning a possible witness." He rested back, the first time his posture had relaxed since he arrived. I was sure my own shoulders wouldn't slide away from their new position, next to my ears, for at least a week. "I didn't see anyone running down the street. Of course, I wasn't really looking and it was dark. The rain was pounding the windshield pretty hard too." He rubbed his chin. "Now that I think back to the drive up here, a car did pass me." He closed his eyes to picture the vehicle. "It was dark and visibility wasn't great, but if I had to guess, I'd say the headlights belonged to a Volkswagen Beetle or a car like that."

My hand flew to my mouth. "I know who it was and I think I've also solved the murders." I hopped up from the couch, newly energized and ready to track down a killer.

"Wait, hold on there, you just had a big scare. Who are we talking about?" He pushed to his feet.

"I need my coat. Gather the flashlights and meet me at the door. I'll tell you all about everything on the way down to the beach." I grabbed my coat and pulled it on.

Briggs picked up a few flashlights but the look on his face was pure confusion. "Why are we heading to the beach on this stormy night?"

"Because I think I know where the murder weapon is hidden. But we have to hurry before she gets away in that rumbling little Volkswagen."

CHAPTER 33

*W*e'd gotten lucky. The weather had shifted downward to a light drizzle, and the thunder and lightning had moved inland. Briggs parked on Pickford Way and we climbed out with our raincoats and flashlights. Neither of us was particularly dressed for a hike on the rocks, but we didn't have time to waste. Briggs had put out the call to keep an eye out for a green Volkswagen, but we hadn't heard any response yet. First, we needed the major piece of evidence, the murder weapon.

"Let me repeat this out loud so I'm understanding all of it," Briggs said as we walked along the wharf. It was a far less inviting place on a wet, dark night. And the clouds had not thinned enough to allow even a stream of moonlight for illumination. "You think this Michael Plesser, the man who was caught cheating a woman out of her life savings, which drove her to suicide, is Lionel Dexter. And the photographer, Heather Houston, is actually Heather Bailey, and her mom was the woman who killed herself."

"Yes, and the fact that Heather seemed to be lying about having a book deal only bolsters my conclusion. She came here pretending to take photos of the lighthouse when she was really just keeping an eye on her victims."

We continued to the staircase leading to the beach.

"But how do you know she was lying about the book deal?" He turned on the flashlight so we could see the steps.

"She told Marty she had a deal with Ballard Publishing, but she told me it was Shuster Publishing. I did some research and neither publisher mentioned any book deal with Heather Houston."

We reached the sand. The storm had produced a white mist over the ocean and wet sand that gave the entire stretch of coast an eerie feel. I wrapped my hand around Briggs' arm. I still hadn't shaken off the major case of nerves from my harrowing evening.

"I have a thousand more questions, but I'll go straight to the most obvious. Why do you think she hid the murder weapon in the rocks?"

"That question has a multilayered response," I said as we trudged through the sand. "Earlier this evening, I decided to head down to the beach to see if I could find out why Heather sent the photos to Kate and Margaret." I realized then that I'd left out a major piece of the puzzle.

Briggs stopped and since I had hold of his arm, I sort of stumbled back. "Heather sent the pictures? How do you know that? And why the heck did my team not know it?"

"It's not their fault. It would have been hard to track down the origin of the photos, but I just happened to see a picture Heather had taken of the lighthouse. She'd printed it on her own printer, which was low on ink. Her blues were sort of green and her blacks were gray." I pulled him along. "We need to find that gun. I got Hilda to let me into the evidence room." I smiled sweetly at him. "I told her you wouldn't mind."

He couldn't argue with that. "So you matched up the colors on the photo in evidence. Very clever, Miss Pinkerton."

"Thank you very much." Even though we were traipsing across a dark beach, headed for a weapon search on slick rocks, I was feeling a million times more myself. "Anyhow, Heather happened to go into Elsie's bakery for a croissant, and she mentioned to Elsie that she had finished with the lighthouse pictures but that she was sticking around for a better shot of the sunset. I know you were stuck in a dreary old courthouse all afternoon, but the sky was clear at dusk. It really was ideal for a sunset photo."

"That storm did move in fast," he noted.

We reached the rocks. Both of us instinctually gazed up at the lighthouse. It looked a little ghostly, almost menacing, in the dark, towering over the rocks with its black hat and one big eye.

"It seems you did exactly what I told you not to do, you confronted a possible murderer," Briggs said as he dragged his gaze downward. "She must have known something was up so she came after you." He held up his hand to stop me from entering my counter argument. "But you did a good job with this one, Lacey." He leaned forward for a quick kiss. "Next time, call me first."

I cleared my throat. "A lot of good that would've done me. You weren't available for most of the day."

He sighed in surrender. "You're right. And I'm sorry."

I kissed him back. "That's all right. You showed up exactly when I needed you most. That was quite the fright. I think I need to teach Kingston to be an attack bird."

He laughed. "Somehow I don't see that happening." He handed me a flashlight, and we aimed our beams at the myriad of rocks in front of us. They looked extra treacherous in the dark, slick with algae and dotted with hidden cracks and crevices.

"I just realized," Briggs said, "you haven't explained to me why we're about to risk our ankles and possible our necks by climbing over these slippery rocks."

"You're right. I got sidetracked. I walked down to the beach just before sunset to look for Heather. There was no sign of her at first. I didn't want to give the impression that I was stalking her, so I took a stroll on the sand as if I'd just come down to the beach for a walk. That's when I spotted Heather. She was coming from the rocks carrying her camera bag. This time her camera was not around her neck," I said excitedly. "That makes sense now."

"You're losing me," Briggs said.

I motioned for him to follow and stepped up on the first rock. He joined me but we split off on different rock paths.

"The first time I met Heather," I continued, "she was taking pictures of Marty in front of the light—eek!" I shrieked and side-stepped an angry crab I'd disturbed with my beam of light. "I forgot about all the crawly things living in these rocks."

"You were talking about the first time you met Heather," Briggs reminded me to get me back on topic.

"Yes, that's right. Well, a wind kicked up and Heather decided to stop the session for the afternoon. She hung the camera around her neck. Marty wisely suggested she put it inside her case but she decided not to. I saw her a few times wearing the camera around her neck and holding onto the camera case. I think she was hiding the gun in her case."

"Clever deduction." He stooped down and aimed his flashlight beam in a crevice.

"Did you find it?" I asked, excitedly.

"Huh? Oh. No, I was just watching this sea urchin. I've only ever seen all these tide pool animals in the day. Kind of interesting to see them at night."

"Detective Briggs, I know you've been cooped up in a courthouse and suit and tie all day but try and concentrate. We're looking for a gun."

He saluted me. "Yes, sir."

Each step took planning and concentration. Once I found a nice solid spot to stand, I circled the flashlight beam around, looking for a flash of metal, anything that was out of place in the rocks. Briggs had his own method. He took a step and circled the flashlight around his body. His was probably the more efficient method but he was far more steady on the rocks than me.

We worked in silence, with only the rhythmic sounds of the ocean for background music. It was an amazingly nice time to be out on the beach, with no other people or sounds to distract from the beauty of nature.

"We should do this more often," I said. "It's kind of cool out here in the dark."

"I was just thinking the same thing." He crouched down. "Hold on.

I think I've got something." In my excitement, I took an enthusiastic step and slipped down to one knee.

Briggs' face popped up. He moved his flashlight beam to his clumsy girlfriend. "Are you all right?" he asked.

"Yes, I'm fine. What did you find?"

He reached into his pocket and pulled out a latex glove. The man was never without his supply of gloves. He pulled it on and his gloved hand disappeared into a crevice. It emerged with a pistol. "Jackpot." He smiled at me. "And all because Lacey Pinkerton is an amazing sleuth. Now, let's go catch a killer."

CHAPTER 34

*W*hat an adrenaline filled night! And it still wasn't over. Briggs got a call that an officer had spotted a green Volkswagen Bug at a gas station in Mayfield. He told the officer to keep his eyes on the car but do nothing until he arrived. We jumped into his car and headed in the direction of Mayfield.

I felt my body press back against the seat as Briggs pressed hard on the pedal. I squealed with excitement. "Can we put the siren on?" I asked.

"No, we don't want to alert her we're on the way."

"Phooey. I'll just have to pretend there's a siren and flashing lights. I'm living out a childhood dream right this moment chasing down a bad guy . . . or woman. I guess I always pictured it was a bad guy because well, let's face it, men just do a lot more bad things."

"Unless they are women who have no qualms about shooting two people point blank," he noted.

"Yes, I'll give you that. Heather Houston, if guilty, which she is, absolutely falls on the side of bad. When you mention two people, it brings me to something that keeps scratching at the back of my mind. Heather obviously killed Lionel because he drove her mother to suicide, but what role do you suppose Glenda played in all this?"

Briggs turned toward the center of Mayfield. "We saw them kiss as he was leaving the boat. It seems she was his true girlfriend and accomplice in his devious schemes. She probably just traveled with him and waited for him to do his thing. Then they both took off with the money and spent it on things like nice boats."

"There's Officer Muir's car." Briggs pointed to a black and white that was sitting at a good distance and, thanks to a delivery truck, out of sight from the gas station.

Briggs picked up his radio. "Officer Muir, this is Detective Briggs, I see the car in question. I want you to stay right where you are, nearby and out of sight."

"Ten four, Detective Briggs. The driver of the vehicle has finished filling her tank. She walked inside the convenience store about five minutes ago."

"Copy that, Muir. Await further instructions. Over." Briggs put down the radio and pulled into the gas station. He parked next to the air pump for tires. His detective car looked like a regular old sedan as long as you didn't look inside of it.

I shot a glimmer of a smile at him, which he caught. "No, you can't use the radio," he said.

"I was just going to give Hilda a quick hello."

"It's past her work hours. Chinmoor is watching her desk. By the way, thank you for insisting that I eat your piece of her coffee cake."

I grinned. "I'm generous to a fault."

"Yes you are. I just can't understand how she can make everything taste so bad. I mean, it seems like you'd have to work hard to make things that flavorless," he said.

I suppressed a giggle. "Poor Hilda and she's always so proud of everything she bakes. I wonder if there's something wrong with her taste buds."

Briggs sat up straighter. "Is this Heather Houston?"

Heather was bundled in a big coat leaving the convenience store with a cup of coffee and a package of mini donuts. "That's her. That's our suspect." I was feeling very official. I reached for the door handle.

"Uh, where do you think you're going?" Briggs asked.

I pointed in the direction of the green car. "I thought I'd help you arrest her."

"Nope," he said curtly. "Stay in the car. She's shot two people and she tried to break down your door. She's dangerous." He climbed out and strode across the gas station lot. He reached for his badge.

I glued my face to the window to watch. If nothing else, at least I had a front row seat to the action. More action than I expected.

"Miss Houston," Briggs called as Heather was climbing into her car.

"Yes?" She peered innocently up over the driver door window.

Briggs flashed his badge. "Detective Briggs of the—" Before he could finish announcing himself, Heather dove into her driver's seat, started the engine and raced a circle around him. I gasped as he jumped out of the way of her car.

He ran back to his own car and jumped inside.

"Oh my gosh, I'm going to be in a real car chase," I chirped.

"Fasten your seat belt, Lacey. This could get wild."

"Gosh, I hope so," I said quietly, really only for my own enjoyment.

Briggs shot me a sideways scowl before he focused his full attention on the road ahead. "Just a good thing it's late enough that the streets are almost empty." We flew down the street behind the Volkswagen. It was going at a pretty good clip considering VW Beetles weren't exactly known for being fast or aerodynamic.

I gripped the edges of my seat as we took a corner so fast, I half expected us to tilt onto two wheels. "Wee," I squeaked. "Sorry, that just called for a wee."

We were heading toward the highway. Even though this was my first real car chase, I was certain letting the suspect's car reach the highway was not a good thing. I glanced in the side view and noticed that the black and white was following quickly at our heels.

"Lacey, hold on. I'm going to try and pass and cut her off." His mouth was pulled in a grim line. I had been acting as if I was on an amusement park ride, but the truth was, this was a dangerous situation.

I double checked my seatbelt and held onto the edge of the seat.

Briggs' car roared as he pushed the pedal to the floor. I was thrown slightly back against the seat. Suddenly, I knew how the astronauts felt in those g-force simulators. Well, sort of.

Tires screeched and the outside world became a blur as we raced past the green car. I flicked my eyes the direction of the speedometer and was sure I saw the dial go past the hundred mark. Once we were clear of Heather's car, Briggs released the gas pedal and swerved in front of her before putting on the brakes. Heather reacted by turning her wheel sharply. Her car bounced up over the curb and rammed straight into a bus bench.

"Stay here and get down in case she found herself another gun," Briggs ordered before jumping out of the car. He pulled his gun from his holster and walked toward Heather's car.

I ducked down but then peered up over the window ledge. I didn't want to miss the action, and since she had only just ditched the murder weapon, it seemed unlikely she had a second one on hand. I definitely hoped so as I watched Briggs walk toward the car, gun positioned in front of him. Back up had arrived and surrounded the car. Heather had no choice except to give up. The driver's side door slowly opened, and she emerged looking as scared as I'd felt just hours earlier when she had rattled my back door.

Briggs ordered her to put her hands on her head. She complied. She had given up. "He deserved to die," she sobbed. "They both did."

CHAPTER 35

$\mathcal{I}$ determined the scene had been secured enough and climbed out of the car. Briggs and another officer were searching Heather's car. Heather was cuffed and being watched over by a female officer as I approached. I almost felt sorry for her. She had gone through an ordeal, and it was easy to see how it might push someone to murder. My sympathy waned some though when her blue eyes shot my direction and her nostrils flared with anger.

"You," she hissed. "This is all your fault. I should've known the first time I met you when that old lighthouse keeper told me you solved murders." Her laugh was mean and edged with hysteria. "I didn't believe him, of course. You don't look as if you could solve a riddle, let alone a murder." My sympathy was vanishing quickly.

I grinned at her. "And yet, here you are standing in handcuffs. Shall I tell you all the mistakes you made? Hmm, let's see," I said before she could respond. "First of all, you shouldn't brag about a pretend book deal. Obviously, you concocted that lie to give yourself cover for hanging around town taking pictures."

The slightest tick had begun to twitch in her cheek. "The lie worked," she sneered. "I had that old lighthouse keeper standing out there for hours, thinking I was there to take pictures of his stupid lighthouse."

"You aren't even a good liar. You gave out two different publisher names. That was my first clue that something wasn't right about your *coffee table* book." I walked a little closer. "And his name is Marty, not old lighthouse keeper, and the Pickford Lighthouse is wonderful. If you were a real artist, you'd see that. But your head was clouded with revenge."

Her icy expression melted some and tears filled her eyes. "Michael Plesser was a monster. My mother was the kindest, most wonderful woman in the world. She trusted everyone. She was funny, outgoing and desperate for love. My father left us when I was seven." A sob bubbled from her throat. "She was devastated and heartbroken. But she rebounded and went to school to become a teacher. The two of us lived a nice, happy life in a small house with our own vegetable garden. Mom was frugal and she socked a lot of money away in retire-ment. It's for you, Heather," she said in a wavering voice. "For you after I'm gone," she continued. My sympathy level was rising again. "She was so in love with him, and she was sure he loved her. I knew there was something strange about him, and I tried to convince her to break it off. Then she started handing him money, everything she had saved. Once it was all gone and she had nothing left to give, he showed up with that *woman*." Her mouth crinkled as if she had just bit into a sour lemon. "Glenda or whatever her real name was. She showed up at our front door in her expensive high heels and fur coat, holding his arm as if they were just going off to be married. He'd come for his things, his clothes, he told my mom. He let her know he was moving out of state and that he never wanted to see her again. My mom didn't eat for days. She got so dehydrated from crying I had to take her to the hospital. She lost her job. That evil man had charged thousands on her credit cards. The bank took the house, the garden." She shrank down with each word until she dropped to her knees to cry. "He only spent a few months in prison," she sobbed. "Our lives were destroyed, but he went right on living the good life." Her head dropped and her shoulders shook.

"I'm sorry," I said quietly. There just wasn't anything else for me to say. I'd been feeling victorious, excited, proud that I'd helped solve the double murder but as I walked back toward Briggs' car, where I intended to sit and get warm, I felt pretty miserable. The justice system hadn't worked the first time, so Heather took matters into her own hands. Listening to her story, it was hard to blame her.

I sat huddled in my own arms, my face buried in the collar of my coat as Briggs finished up. The police put Heather into the back of the squad car for transportation to the precinct. Briggs walked back to his car and climbed in. Being a wonderful boyfriend, he instantly sensed that something was off.

He took hold of my hand. "I saw you talking to Heather. Are you all right?"

I sniffled to assure him I wasn't. "Maybe I shouldn't have pursued this one. But I didn't know the motive." I swiped at a tear and turned to him. Again, wonderful boyfriend and friend that he was, he just listened instead of talking me out of my notions. "It was a really good motive. I don't know what I'd do if someone destroyed my mom's life, driving her to suicide. It all seems justified. The system didn't work for her. Michael Plesser committed terrible crimes and got almost no jail time."

Briggs reached across for an awkward hug over the console. It was still effective. I always felt better with his arms around me. "I know it doesn't seem fair, Lacey, but she killed two people. She played judge, jury and executioner in this." He straightened. "As rotten as the two victims might have been, they didn't deserve this."

I nodded, reluctantly. "You're right, of course." I sniffled again. "I guess that's why I wouldn't make a great detective. I let my emotions get in the way."

"Wrong, a good detective always keeps that human side handy. It's just as important as the cold, official side. And the way you ferreted out this suspect, with no help from the police, was nothing short of amazing. I'm proud of you, Miss Pinkerton." He leaned over for a kiss. That darn console was in the way again.

"I've realized something with this last case," I said. "Sometimes it's better to just have a pair of eyes and ears hanging around town. It's amazing what you can discover just talking to the lighthouse keeper or visiting the local bakery. But don't forget, I did have one visit to the evidence room to look at the photo. I just got lucky when the print quality matched the quality of Heather's lighthouse photo."

"Which you wouldn't have seen if you hadn't been *hanging around town.*"

"Yep, my point, exactly."

"Well, I'm starved," Briggs said. "How about dropping by Franki's for some late night pancakes?"

"Yes, after this evening, I think I deserve some pancakes."

CHAPTER 36

$\mathcal{I}$ stuck the herbal remedy handbook into a plastic bag in case it rained on our hike up to the Hawksworth house. The old book with its yellowed pages had belonged to Marty's mother. She had kept it with her few treasures, so I needed to take good care of it.

Briggs put on his fedora and picked up the umbrella I pulled out for our walk. We opened the front door of my house and we were pelted with cold windblown drops of rain. The sky was so dark, it could have been midnight rather than three in the afternoon.

"Tell me again, why are we walking in the rain up the hill to that dilapidated old house when we could be right here, snuggled on the couch, watching movies?" Briggs asked.

"I told you I have something very important to do, and this is a good time. The rain means no one else will be up there." I pushed open the umbrella. His big hand wrapped around mine when a gust of wind nearly took me off on a Mary Poppins' style flight.

We headed down my driveway. "So we're going to be breaking into the gardener's shed to snoop around in dusty artifacts."

"Boy, you get kind of grumpy when you don't get your snuggle and movie time in," I said.

"You bet I do." His arm slid around my back, and he squeezed me closer to his side as he held the umbrella over his head. "Guess I'll have to steal some snuggle time right now under the umbrella."

I inched even closer to him. "It is kind of romantic, walking in the rain, sharing an umbrella."

"Can't think of any other person on this earth I'd rather share an umbrella with," he said.

The sharp climb up to Maple Hill was considerably harder in the cold drizzle and intermittent wind. Briggs had to use both hands to keep the umbrella from taking off like a jet fueled kite. Once we reached the site, the wind was gusting around the house, and we were taking a less direct hit.

"Just like you said, no one comes up here in the rain," he noted.

We stopped and gazed up at the empty house. It grew more dilapidated and looked considerably more haunted with each visit. The dark, brooding sky behind it only added to the dark, grim look of the home.

We circled around to the gardener's shed, where the town kept the few treasured artifacts left behind in the manor. Given the tragic and macabre events that took place in the home just over a century earlier, the artifacts were a big tourist attraction. I personally found them lacking. I'd been the only person to have the privilege of viewing the contents of Bertram Hawksworth's personal trunk. It was the only relic in the shed with anything worth looking at.

I pulled on the permanently broken lock and took the flashlight out of my pocket. The dank, musty smell built up inside the shed was overpowering. I sneezed three times and waited for a fourth, but it seemed my nose had gotten used to the smell.

Briggs held the flashlight for me as I dropped to my knees and searched blindly beneath the trunk for the secret key compartment. It dropped into my palm, and I opened the lock.

"As a member of the police force, I'm going to forget everything I saw here today," Briggs said wryly.

"That's probably best. Now kneel down here next to me. I'm going to need your police force expertise in a second."

Briggs knelt down next to me. We opened the lid of the trunk, and I reached in for the letters. I pulled out one of Button's love letters to Teddy. Then I took out the herbal handbook with Jane's handwritten note to Elizabeth Tate.

"This book belongs to Marty. It was his mother's. Jane Price gave it to her, and she wrote a little note to her on the title page. If my hunch is right and it's still just a big hunch, then the handwriting in this book will match the love letters written to Bertram Hawksworth." I opened the creaky book cover to Jane's inscription. Then I carefully unfolded one of the letters.

"Do you think Jane Price was having a love affair with Bertram Hawksworth?" James asked. He positioned the flashlight beam so it glowed over the book and letter.

"Yes, that's my hunch, and there's more to it than that. But first let's compare the writing."

We both studied the handwriting for a good, long minute. The inscription was more hastily written, almost as an afterthought, whereas the letter looked as if it had been lovingly produced with a fresh pen dip for each word. Yet, there were similarities.

"Here." Briggs pointed to the capital T on both the letter and the book. "See this fancy curlicue at the end of the T? That is a unique way to write the letter T, and it appears on both handwriting samples."

"True but I wish it was more of a match. The book is sort of sloppy and scrawled, but the letter writer took more time."

"Each written under different circumstances. My writing looks way different on my reports than it does on my grocery list." He waved his finger over the letter. "See the slant and the size and shape of the letter? They are similar. I wouldn't say it's a hundred percent, but I think you might have a match."

"I suppose you're right. I think I'm on the right track anyhow. Marty also had a picture of Jane Price, and while the clothes didn't make it easy to see the baby bump, I'm almost certain that she was pregnant in the photo." I folded up the letters and placed them back into the trunk, then I placed the book back into its plastic bag.

We locked up the trunk, and I returned the key back to its secret compartment. Briggs offered me his hand and popped me to my feet. We landed together *accidentally*.

"I kind of like the name Button," Briggs said. "Maybe I should start calling you that."

I squinted. "How about I just write you the occasional text signed off as Button?"

"Does that mean a love letter is out?" he asked.

We walked out and I held the umbrella as he *locked* up the shed.

"Actually, writing love letters should never have gone out of style." I took his arm. "But since I don't have pad and paper handy, I'll just recite one to you."

"Dear James, My love, My handsome detective, My—well, you get the picture.

So often I wake up and the first thing that pops into my head is your name. Well, occasionally the words Elsie's chocolate croissant comes first, but I promise you, my dear boyfriend, that your name pops up a close second. I would also like to thank you for putting up with my idiosyncrasies, my ridiculous sense of smell and the occasional sneeze fits that come with it and with my constant curiosity that quite often gets me into trouble. On that line of thought, thank you for somehow managing always to be there right when I need you the most. Which feels like all the time, lately, James Briggs."

I stopped and turned to him under the shelter of our shared umbrella. His brown eyes glittered with amusement and what I quickly convinced myself was total, abject love. "In conclusion, my love, thank you for coming into my life."

"Believe me, Lacey Pinkerton." He wrapped his arm around me and pulled me closer. "The pleasure is all mine." We kissed under the umbrella in the middle of a rainstorm. Most romantic kiss ever.

CARAMEL CHOCOLATE BONBONS

View recipe online at londonlovett.com/recipe-box

Caramel Chocolate
BONBONS

Ingredients:

Filling:

-12-14 fresh dates
-1 Tbsp almond butter (or other nut butter)
-1 tsp vanilla

Toppings:

-6 oz of dark chocolate
-shredded coconut
-flake salt
-crushed pistachios

Directions:

1. Remove pits from the dates. If they seem dry, you can soak the dates in boiling water for 5 minutes and then drain before using.

2. Combine dates, almond butter (or other nut butter) and vanilla in a food processor. Pulse until the ingredients are combined into a sticky caramel like mixture.

3. Using a tablespoon or cookie scoop, scoop the date caramel mixture onto a parchment paper lined dish.

4. Allow the balls of caramel to set in the freezer for 30 minutes or until firm.

5. Prep your toppings. We used shredded coconut, crushed pistachios and a little flake salt, but you can get creative here. Choose your favorite toppings!

6. Melt dark chocolate in a double boiler or in the microwave. Be careful not to overcook the chocolate. If using the microwave, heat for 30 seconds at a time, stirring in between. Once a good portion is melted you can stop heating and stir the rest of the chocolate until melted.

7. Remove caramels from the freezer, dip them in chocolate, and sprinkle with toppings. You'll need to work quickly here, and yes, it's going to get messy. Once coated, return the parchment lined dish of finished chocolates to the freezer for 30 minutes or until firm. Candies can be kept in the refrigerator once hardened.

8. ENJOY!

There will be more from Port Danby soon. In the meantime, check out my new Starfire Cozy Mystery series! Books 1 & 2 are now available.

Los Angeles, 1923. The land of movie stars and perpetual sunshine has a stylish new force to be reckoned with—**Poppy Starfire,** *Private Investigator.*

See all available titles: LondonLovett.com

ABOUT THE AUTHOR

London Lovett is the author of the Port Danby, Starfire and Firefly Junction Cozy Mystery series. She loves getting caught up in a good mystery and baking delicious, new treats!

Join London Lovett's Secret Sleuths!:
facebook.com/groups/londonlovettssecretsleuths/

Subscribe to London's newsletter at www.londonlovett.com to never miss an update.

London loves to hear from readers. Feel free to reach out to her on Facebook: Facebook.com/londonlovettwrites, Follow on Instagram: @londonlovettwrites, Or send a quick email to londonlovettwrites@gmail.com.

Made in the USA
Monee, IL
15 August 2020